ROUND THE FIRESIDE

With

Sherlock Holmes
(Certain Favourite Cases)

By

Spike Brown

**Round the Fireside
With Sherlock Holmes**

Contents

That Awful Hat

"**M**R SHERLOCK HOLMES?" A red-head girl came wheeling her bicycle over to the churchyard wall.

"I am he," said my companion, stepping forward and shaking her delicate, gloved hand.

"Oh, thank goodness. We were told by Mrs Lawson, who owns the holiday let, that you and Dr Watson were up from London. We are in desperate need of your opinion," said she, breathlessly.

"Do go on."

"It's that old duffer, Carlton, up at the manor. The Major hates us like billy-o for using his footpath to ride our bicycles along, and he's complained to the village committee that we never ring our bells properly and that we startled his damned stupid little pooch. Yapping and snarling and biting at our ankles, it was, that's more like the truth!" she said hurriedly, her apple-blossom cheeks flushing delightfully.

"Is it his land?" enquired my colleague, taking out his pipe, matches and tobacco pouch.

"It's everybody's. The path is used by umpteen of the villagers, and has been forever. Well, I will say Florrie dropped her bonnet along his footpath. I think it was near the iron gate. Like us, she was pedalling furiously and a breath of breeze set it scuttling off. We were so anxious to get away from that horrid, red-faced old man with his shotgun, our mob pressed on to the main road and her bonnet just got left behind in some ditch. Nobody's fault."

"Indeed. Was it of some value?"

"Just a plain, ordinary straw bonnet, Mr Holmes. The sort we girls wear in summer."

"Of course, pray continue."

"Well, amazingly, the next morning Florrie's mother finds it on the porch step - the bonnet, I mean. Someone had returned it. Oh crikey, Mr Holmes, by_ the afternoon she was dead! Florrie died at ten past two. She passed away in her bedroom."

"My dear young lady, you are still a trifle inexperienced so far as worldly matters are concerned. Alas, we shall all of us pass away at some time."

"But the hat," she cried. "The hat, Mr Holmes, she became ill after putting on the bonnet! Did he curse it?"

"Now, calm down," said I. "You blame a straw hat for your friend's sudden fatal illness. Surely that's a trifle eccentric!"

"Oh Lord, I'm sorry, Dr Watson. I mean, can a man curse somebody, like witches?" she asked in a determined way. "It's just all so peculiar how her face and feet swelled up. One day Florrie's a member of our cycle club, a crowd of us pedalling across the Downs, carefree and gay, the next she's passed away and to be buried in the churchyard."

"Here in Pulborough?"

"Yes. Daft old Whitty, the sexton,' s been busy preparing a grave for her. It's so unfair."

"Well, anyhow, Dr Watson and I are delighted to meet you all," exclaimed my companion. "Would you care to introduce us, Miss ... ?"

"Oh, Tometi, Tometi Stevens. There are nine of us. Oops, I mean eight now Florrie's gone. Amy, Jessi, Edie, Ems, Aggs, Prune, Dots and me."

The young ladies smiled enthusiastically and nodded in our direction.

I observed some splendid bicycles amongst them - a Raleigh, Rovers and Townsend Coventry tourers. The ladies wore practical sporting clothing: blouses with leg-of-mutton sleeves and uniform long, chocolate- brown skirts and bonnets. But this collection of young ladies had not cycled to the church merely to look pretty and engaging.

"Florrie was murdered," said the girl Ems, leaning her bike defiantly against the old sun-drenched stone walling. "She was, Mr Holmes. We're not sure exactly how, but she was murdered."

"By that beastly old Major."

"Old duffer Carlton."

"Well," said our magistrate friend, Phelps, pitching in. "I'm not that keen on Major Carlton either, but I should draw the line at calling him a murderer. An old army man, certainly a landowner, but not a murderer. An 'old duffer' is one thing, but you mustn't confuse the two. Your club was, in our official jargon, 'trespassing', my dears. The footpath is the major's right-of-way. All right, no one cares and we all use it, but it's on his land. I mean, perhaps he threatened you with a shotgun, but I doubt if he'd actually be prepared to use it."

"You should have seen the major pointing his gun at us, chasing after us with that sniping, growling rat-catcher of a dog snapping at our heels," said Tometi, flicking her flame-coloured hair and turning to leave.

That evening was spent quietly reading or catching up on case notes. How pleasant not to bear the heat and stuffiness of London. I believe it was one of the hottest Julys on record in the city and we were glad to be out of it for a fortnight or so.

I was for an early bed and I went into my room leaving Holmes to potter about, extinguish the oil lamps and lock up. The clean country air down here suited healthy living wonderfully, and made one feel pleasantly tired after the day's exertions.

I thought of Tometi, such an energetic and persistent young girl. But murder was a very serious allegation, and from long experience and watching Holmes deal with the very worst of villains, many of whom were regarded as perfectly respectable types, hanged on evidence provided by my colleague, I felt she had better watch her step in future. To accuse someone simply because you did not like them was not enough. Young people were always apt to be impetuous, anyhow.

––––––––

"What on earth has happened?" said I, letting Tometi, the redhead, into our holiday flat the following morning. Ham and eggs were sizzling in the pan I had earlier placed upon the hob in our modest kitchenette, the greasy haze of frying bacon blending with wreaths of tobacco smoke coiling from Holmes' long pipe. He sat smoking contentedly in his dressing gown perusing The Times, a languid, droopy-lidded expression upon his features.

"Oh, it's nothing." She smiled sweetly, placing a brown paper bag overflowing with ripe and softened damsons upon the table, fresh from her garden.

"But your finger is swollen. Here, let me take a look. Bluey-black, Holmes, rather similar to a nasty wasp sting."

"Poisonous - better lance it, Watson."

"Yes, I'll stick this sewing needle over the gas to cauterise it. Tometi, are you allergic to insect bites or wasp stings? Hurry, think, Miss Stevens. Are you in pain?"

"Old duffer Carlton's the only pain round here," she answered mischievously.

"Do you feel faint? Lethargic?"

"A little."

"Not shivery?"

"No, Mr Holmes." The girl hooted with laughter." All this fuss. Oh, it's in my bag, by the way."

"What is, Miss Stevens?" asked Holmes, looking at her in his searching fashion.

"The bonnet."

"Not that again. Really, your sheer gall and persistence impresses me." Then his face suddenly darkened. "Don't touch it," said he, "either of you. You handled that straw hat this morning, presumably, Miss Stevens. But did not place it on your head."

"No, why should I? I have my own hat. Oh, and I found out there are men who can curse, by the way. Cast spells. Warlocks, they're called. Is the major a warlock, I wonder? A fat old curmudgeon like that, I ask you!"

"Do stop prattling on about such nonsense, Tometi. Let me fix your finger. Here, I'll put some iodine on it and bandage it for you. You can stay for breakfast, if you like," said I.

"Miss Stevens, you are certain you did not place the hat on your head when you perchance glanced in the hall mirror as young ladies are wont to do of a morning?"

"Pshaw! I told you, Mr Holmes, I put it straight in my cloth bag. Florrie's mother gave it to· me as a little keepsake to remind me of my friend. Oh dear, I'm going to start crying again, sobbing my eyes out in a minute. They're burying her up at the church this morning, you know."

Holmes had located a pair of tweezers and, leaning his tall, gangly frame over the kitchen table, plucked the straw bonnet by the brim and, always careful not to let it touch any part of his exposed skin, removed it from Tometi's bag.

"I imagine your finger swelled up when cycling over here on your Rover Tourer," he commented.

"Mr Holmes, I wondered if perhaps I'd bruised it grabbing the handlebars when I got onto my bicycle before saying goodbye to Mama."

"No, young lady, you pricked it," my companion elaborated. "Upon closer inspection of this damned clever hat, I extracted from the crown a most singular barbed insect stinger belonging to a large hornet woven into the inner lining and held securely in place with a liberal dab of cow glue."

"How disgusting!" shrieked Tometi accusingly, her pretty, freckled face turning bright red. "It's the major's doing. Old duffer Carlton's to blame."

"Miss Stevens," said Holmes, with a calm, detached air, "you will excuse my presumption, but this poisonous hornet's stinger undoubtedly caused your friend's death. When Florrie put it on her head, placing her hands either side of the brim, the top of the hat pressing downwards upon her scalp would have caused a scratch, a tiny sting that would have barely registered. According to you, Miss Stevens, she became ill shortly afterwards. By Jove, Watson, this was no warlock's curse, rather a practical invention. A steady hand should have been required to affix the insect stinger so firmly."

Suddenly the door burst open. It was our friend, the local magistrate, Rodney Phelps.

"Good morning, gentlemen. There are the remains of a fort on a mound west of the railway, possibly a catapulter used by a vigilant Roman garrison against the invader. Are you up for a hike and then lunch in the village?"

"Not at present," said my companion seriously, whilst I shared out the fried rashers and eggs after reheating the pan.

"Ah, well, be seeing you both later, no doubt," the impatient fellow replied before hurrying off.

After pouring us hot coffee, I was relieved that, despite her swollen finger, Miss Stevens was possessed of a healthy appetite and appeared very chirpy and bullish. She recounted many amusing tales concerning her club of young lady cyclists. However, at the end of our meal, refilling my briar pipe once I had taken my seat in the corner, I was determined that we should proceed with extreme sensitivity and caution.

"We must keep a steady ship on this," said I, scratching away with a vesta. "On no account, Tometi, are you to approach the major. Start throwing allegations willy-nilly at him and he could perfectly well take you to court, and that would not please your dear mother, I'm sure. Allow Mr Holmes to decide what steps to take. Don't do anything rash and act on your own impulse. Understood?"

She hurriedly ate a piece of crusty loaf and nodded.

"The Major's seriously potty," she managed to say between mouthfuls. "An absolute stinker. I'm off to Florrie's funeral, anyhow."

—

The funeral for Florrie Hepworth took place over at Pulborough Parish Church at 11 a.m. and was well attended. Most poignant was the number of safety and touring bicycles propped in a row against the churchyard wall.

At this early juncture, neither Holmes nor I were entirely convinced Major Carlton was the guilty party. After all, the mislaid straw hat could quite easily have been snatched by someone else lurking near the footpath that day. It might be said that a person does not attain the rank of major by being a total buffoon. Having been an army man myself; part of the British regimental system, I rarely encountered a totally stupid high-ranking officer. I should disagree, or become infuriated, with their campaign strategy, certainly, but dismiss them as an 'old duffer', certainly not. Tometi had, in her youthful exuberance, perhaps severely underestimated him and his ability to go to law should her allegations be unfounded and he, as a consequence, slandered.

Further along the street we stopped off at the village post office. My companion was anxious to despatch a telegram to his elder brother, Mycroft, who, as a key consultant to Her Majesty's government, would have been privy to details of the major's army career before his retirement via Whitehall and a whole host of military bureaucracy.

At the time, I was more concerned with purchasing a two ounce tin of my favourite Ships tobacco and I took my place in the queue.

"Damn and blast," I heard a bluff old bespectacled chap say with an air of truculence. He sneezed and blew his purplish nose, which was both bulbous and veined, into his hanky. He wore a Norfolk jacket and knickerbockers in the style of a gamekeeper. I instantly took him to be an ex-army man.

"Lost me bloomin' wallet. Ah, here we are. Box of my usual coronas, Mrs Teal. Dashed hot weather we' re having, eh?"

"Oh, indeed, Major Carlton. They tells me in Lunnon the temperature's unbearable. My sister wrote to me from Ealing complaining the tarmacadam along her street was meltin' - meltin', I ask you. That'll be two shillin's and fourpence, Major. Will you be attendin' the annual committee meeting over at the vicarage? Mr Phelps the magistrate tells me there is much to be discussed concerning boundary issues."

"Yes, I've had a dashed lot of bother recently: D' you know, I was walking along my own footpath when I nearly got run down by that ruddy ladies' cycle club. A whole brigade of 'em! Must have been doing ten miles an hour at least. Forced me into the bloody ditch, nearly killed my dog. I had my huntin' gun under me arm, so I pointed twin barrels at 'em and told 'em to clear off my land, what!"

"Ha, ha, I'd love to have seen their faces, Major. We don't want none of them young cyclists runnin' us over, do we? Modem fad, so unladylike. What's the world comin' to? Never used to go on."

"Good mornin', gentlemen, didn't see you there in the sunlight. Are you up here on holiday?" said the amenable old fellow, reaching out to shake my hand.

"Marylebone is scorching," said I. "It's the hottest July I can remember."

"India's got nothing on this heat, old boy," he admitted. "And to think I served out there with my regiment for over twenty years. Dealing with the

Dervishes, damned uprising an' all. Well, good day to you both. Cheerio, Mrs Teal."

"Can you really, in truth, imagine that old chap, who must be seven and sixty at least, and by his beetroot complexion loves his beef, port, brandy and cigars, having the latent ability to create a means of killing a young lady by tampering with her hat?" said I, incredulously.

"I grant you, my dear Watson," replied my companion, stepping out of the shade afforded by the post office shop into the unbearably bright, sweltering noonday heat, "it seems highly improbable."

We headed back to the blessed cool of our holiday let and flaked out. Slumped in the corner, sipping my glass of India pale ale, I was surprised to see our magistrate friend, Rodney Phelps, bound through the door not ten minutes after we arrived home. He entered our small kitchenette in a state of considerable excitement, waving a tiny package about.

"Major Carlton . . . asked me to give you this," he chuckled. "When I told him the great detective, Sherlock Holmes, and his biographer, Dr Watson, were holed up in Mrs Lawson's holiday flat, he could not believe it He has read all of your adventures in *The Strand* magazine. A slight, ah, problem, though. The girl Tometi cycled over to the manor last night and accused him of putting a curse on Florrie's straw hat, of being a confounded warlock. Furthermore, and I regret to say this, gentlemen, she really got his back up when she more than hinted that yourself and Dr Watson here had been employed by the cycle club to bring him to summary justice and see that he hangs for murder."

"Dear me," said Holmes, charging up his clay, "that's dropped us in very deep water. The Major must have been most put out. Anyhow, what's that package you're holding?"

"Well, he asked me to give it to you. A present, I think. You know, it's a bit unfair, Torneti coming down on him like a ton of bricks. He was wounded out of the army and misses his chums terribly.

Young people have absolutely no idea how much we owe the likes of him. I don't know what this generation's coming to. I mean, I can understand young fellows taking to bicycles, but ladies - no, that's wrong. It goes against the female temperament. I mean, just look at that lot we've got tearing round Pulborough - nine of 'em, all come whizzing along the High Street, nearly run you down and have the audacity to talk back to you as though you're a blessed moron."

By now, Sherlock Holmes had ripped open the package. He held the object up to the light of the window.

"A meerschaum pipe. I'm more of a briar-root man, myself. But I expect it'll smoke well enough."

"I say, are you gentlemen up for a walk to the old Roman fort? I've been sketching all morning."

"What, in this heat?" said I, incredulously. "Leave the catapulter site until later this evening, when it's cooler.

"Very well, Dr Watson. I shall call for you fellows at around seven. We shall take advantage of the local hostelry then."

Our friend departed, promising to buy us a pint of beer each at The Stag later.

"Put that pipe up on the windowsill, will you Watson? I might try it later, although I'm not too keen on the meerschaum, myself."

————

Later, the loud rap of the telegram boy disturbed me from my nap. He arrived bearing an official form. I straightaway handed the telegram over to Holmes, who was slouching over a newspaper, smoking a cigarette.

"An answer to your enquiry from Mycroft," said I. "Thank you, Watson. Pour us a stiff whisky, will you? Humph, dear, dear me. It appears Miss Steven's intense suspicions concerning Major Carlton are highly justified."

"How so?"

"Because, my dear fellow, Mycroft informs us that the major was a bomb disposal officer, highly decorated."

"I don't follow."

"Surely a fellow who can defuse an explosive device, defeat its intricate mechanism, penetrate the core of its diabolical clockwork, is more than qualified to attach a poisoned hornet's stinger to the inside of a hat!"

"My God, Holmes, I can see what you're driving at, but he is an older fellow now."

"The habits of a lifetime's career in the military are not easily lost. My goodness, what's that horrid smell, Watson?"

The pipe I had earlier placed on the windowsill was now smouldering, acrid grey fumes filling the kitchenette.

"It's a bomb, Watson. For heaven's sake, sling it out of the window."

I leapt up, toppling over my chair, charged towards the open window and, grabbing the pipe, hurled it as far as it would go out into the garden. We heard a loud 'crump' as it exploded amongst Mrs Lawson's rose bushes.

We were both of us incensed, despairing, even, that anybody could have, through sheer spite, wished to inflict a severe facial injury over the simple action of striking a match and lighting one's pipe, that most manly and pleasurable of everyday activities with which we are, all of us, so familiar.

The pipe-bomb, a meerschaum with a curved, amber stem, the bowl shaped in the face of the composer Franz Liszt, had been adapted to form an explosive device detonated using a heat source. In this case, the summer sun had reflected off the windowpane and intensified further as it shone through the cut glass of a crystal flower vase placed on the sill, creating a lens effect, causing the fuse in the pipe to ignite, the ensuing fumes warning us of the danger in time.

"It is he," my companion exclaimed, disgusted at the low trick, jumping up with a passion before seizing his hat and cane and heading for the door.

"Something must have snapped with the major. Why should a highly decorated, brave army chap like that act so irrationally?"

"He should be publicly stripped of his medals." I confess my temper got the better of me." Anyhow, his manor is but a short distance from the parish church." I took a further cautionary glance outside at the garden before we left. "That rascal shall have some explaining to do."

"Have you your service revolver handy, Watson?"

"I have it here, old man."

"Capital. We are bound to inform the local coroner that an exhumation must be arranged post-haste. I'll wager the young lady from the cycle club was killed by that dratted hat, the hornet's stinger immersed in some execrable venomous poison, a derivative of a deadly snake found in only certain provinces of India, no doubt. It is obvious Major Carlton now regards us as a real threat to his liberty. This murderous behaviour bears all the hallmarks of a basically 'decent sort' gone badly off the rails. I propose a recurring fever brought on in the Tropics when on active service affected his reason."

"Excusing his proclivity for murder just won't do," said I. "That blasted pipe could have disfigured you for life, Holmes. I'll see him hang."

———————

The Major's property was an old-fashioned gabled house set in a large, evergreen-hedged garden on the outskirts of Pulborough village. From the church, we took a brisk trudge up a path leading across some arable fields - the footpath where that unfortunate girl from the cycle club suffered the misfortune of mislaying her hat while out riding with Tometi and her friends. The girls had paid dearly for their breezy and innocent trespass, for out of an overriding sense of anger and outrage that he and his dog had nearly been shoved into a ditch and that the path on his own land was being used as a cycle route by a group of high-spirited, pretty young ladies, he saw fit to murder one of them. A ridiculously spiteful reaction, an action one could only attribute not to an aggrieved landowner, but surely a fevered madman!

I furiously tugged at the bell pull. Moments later, an elderly housekeeper, a small, alert woman, hunched over and rubbing her hands, appeared at the door.

"Where is he?" My companion chafed with impatience. "Kindly summon your master at once."

"Are you gentlemen the physicians, perchance?" said she, arching her heavily-tufted eyebrows in surprise. "I've just sheeted him. And where's Dr Crabbe?"

"The devil - I am a consulting detective, madam. We are here on an urgent matter concerning the gift of a 'joke shop' meerschaum pipe and a filthy, cold-blooded murder. Fetch the major, I wish to have words. It's deuced serious!"

"Too late," the prim and proper creature replied with a frown, smacking her gums.

"I suppose he's made a run for it, eh?" said my colleague petulantly, tapping the tip of his cane upon the granite step, presuming the hunt for our fox might prove much more of a chase than expected.

"Lor', bless us, sir, Major Carlton won't be going nowhere. He passed on some twenty minutes ago," she told us plain. "Sunk into his leather armchair with a deep sigh an' none of us have been able to raise him since. The old malaria to which he was prone may have had something to do with his death, according to cook. He just wasn't himself this last week or so."

Hearing raised voices, a crowd of gossipy maids had gathered in the hall, their heads cocked at an insolent angle. Despite the housekeeper's protestations, Holmes and I pushed past and lost no time carrying out a search of the lower ground floor. The Major himself did not object to this unwarranted intrusion of his manor. He sat before the hearth, his corpulent frame sheeted like a ghost.

We found his study to be predominantly filled with angling clutter - nets, fishing rods, reels and tackle boxes - but there was a glass-lidded cabinet displaying pinned insects - butterflies, moths, wasps, bees and a variety of winged hornets.

The old oak desk, at which he had no doubt spent many hours conspiring and inventing, was festooned with an array of tiny, intricate instruments, a number of split-open 'No. 5' cartridge cases, cotton wadding, a powerful eyeglass and, more damning still, the stale vapours left by a spirit lamp with a pot of boiled cow glue on top, the gum brush still stuck to the insides of a congealed mess of resin.

—————————

Later that afternoon, we joined our friend Rodney Phelps, an avid student of prehistory, for a trudge up to the old catapulter site.

"Shame about old Carlton popping his clogs like that," said he." A heart failure, the hot weather blamed. Not surprising. I believe this is the hottest July since records began in England. Do tell me what you think about this splendid hill fort, Holmes.

The inhabitants dropped a large number of coins, many of which have been dug up."

"A very notable ruin," my colleague agreed, puffing on his pipe.

Discovery at Kew

I AM NOT NORMALLY A PARTICULARLY EARLY RISER and find it irksome to be disturbed from slumber, denied the simple pleasure of awaking by my own volition.

This was to be my lot when Inspector Lestrade took it upon himself to knock up our lady housekeeper at half past four in the morning, causing a volley of complaints to be directed at me and Mr Sherlock Holmes as we clattered down the staircase and made our way through the front door to the waiting cab. Wearing her nightdress, Mrs Hudson stood in the hall, sternly admonishing us, hair in disarray, lamp in hand, the unflattering shadows it cast making her appear like a veritable Medusa.

"Well," said I, joining my companion and the Scotland Yard detective. "That's going to take a week at least to clear the air! I cannot abide it when Mrs Hudson is displeased with us, Holmes. My nerves won't stand it. I should not like to be turfed out on the street with all my worldly possessions and forced to find other digs if you don't mind, Lestrade."

Holmes appeared far from supportive, merely striking a match to his pipe, peering intently at the gloomy facades of the shops and double-fronted houses opposite, the yellow glimmer of the gas lamps reflected on the gleaming surface of the road.

"Now, now," said our Scotland Yarder, buttoning up his coat. "Women are such strangely mercurial creatures, Dr Watson, who soon forget and forgive our little foibles. I'll warrant she'll be her old cheery self once you've returned from Kensington in need of a hearty breakfast."

"Kensington?" I queried, searching in my coat pocket for my pipe and pouch of Arcadia mixture. "Has a town house been burgled, then?"

"My dear fellow," my companion puffed avidly on his briar-root pipe, "Lestrade presents us with an intriguing problem -a first for the botanical gardens at Kew, I believe, Inspector."

"Indeed," he replied in all seriousness. "We are presently dealing with the recovery of a body, Dr Watson, and a most queer place to find one, I must say."

Some time later, we were shepherded away from a large glass hothouse and conservatory, taking a pathway across the park towards the thickly wooded south-western section at Kew. Dawn was breaking over London and I confess I was at a complete loss as to the body's whereabouts until I observed a mass of crows squawking and bickering above the tree canopy. We joined a group of police officers, Kew officials and groundsmen who, with glowing faces, gazed purposefully heavenward at the sprawling branches of a tall oak tree growing amongst the horse chestnut, leafy silver birches and alder thereabouts.

A constable had climbed up the wide trunk and was securing a rope and pulley to what appeared to be a bamboo platform strung high up in the branches. At least, despite the attack of birds, he succeeded and a recovery, of sorts, took place.

"Bring it down gently," the sergeant of police cried through a loudhailer. "Patiently does it, Davies, don't make the damn thing wobble so. Tug more on the left rope, less on the right. Keep it level, for gawd' s sake. How's the body bearing up?"

"Badly pecked, sir," bellowed the other from a great height, accompanied by the sound of creaking, dripping branches. "Darn big those rooks, too. I reckon every crow in London's wound up here at Kew."

The makeshift platform, basically bamboo poles roped together, was lowered to the ground and at last we were able to gather round. A shrouded bundle lay secured to the top of the platform by means of dried palm fronds twisted and knotted together. The face of the deceased was concealed by an oriental decorative face mask, much damaged by the incessant pecking of the crows. The shroud was pocked with tears and rips in the cloth, the material itself dirtied and smudged mossy green from having been up in the canopy for so long.

Holmes lost no time in examining the bamboo struts and bindings with his magnifying lens before turning his attention to the reclining cadaver. Lestrade and I eagerly joined my colleague, kneeling beside him on the dewy, tussocky grass. We helped cut away the matted shroud.

"Hum, upon the thigh I observe clear evidence of bite marks long healed, presumably from snakes, else poisonous insects. See upon the calves and ankles -scarring to the skin tissue caused by greedy leeches clinging on. By Jove, this fellow evidently· spent much of his working life wading through rice paddy fields, or enduring long treks through the jungle; an explorer, perhaps? But I should favour our obvious links with Kew - a plant hunter, an experienced one, too. On removing the mask, the face appears too badly pecked to identify. Now, Watson, will you assist me in unfolding a little more of this sorry, tangled shroud to free his arm? Ah, we can safely detect from this deep indentation upon the third finger of his right hand the mark of a wide signet ring. More light, if you please, Inspector. See how the ring has been energetically prised off, else cut away with pliers. So, in life, the fellow wore this ring without hardly ever removing it. It was a deuced tight fit, hence the swollen knuckle joint. The inference of the tree burial is not entirely lost to me - the funerary rites practised by peoples from as diverse regions as India and Nepal to Bali and Lornbok. The exact origin of the decorative mask escapes me."

"Good gracious, sir," exclaimed a gentleman wearing a bowler hat and tweeds, a florid-faced chap with mutton-chop whiskers and piercing eyes. He drew closer with his storm lantern, his mouth hanging open in disbelief. "You've practically described the man I know so well. This is my dear friend and fellow botanist, Cuthbert Glenny. The last I heard he was off to Bali in search of rare orchids. The Asprey ring was a gift from his sweetheart, Miss Violet Dunnwiddy, the daughter of the coal magnate Rawlings Dunnwiddy of Yorkshire. It was a token of her love and Cuthbert rarely took it off. They were to be married in Rudston. What a damn travesty."

"Is there nothing remotely suspicious about this wretched business, then?" asked Lestrade, getting up and brushing himself down. "No foul play suspected, Mr Holmes?"

"To summarise, by a process of natural decomposition and the consumption of the body by your busy London crow population, it is difficult to determine whether the plant hunter was murdered or not." My colleague lit a cigarette. "Well, my dear Watson, there is nothing more we can do here. I suggest we return to our rooms at Baker Street and, in more civilised sur-roundings, enjoy a breakfast of rashers and egg. I am absolutely famished. Inspector, I shall wire Scotland Yard once I have had more time to consider the facts. Oh, and if you don't mind, I shall borrow this ferocious looking mask for a while. Good morning, Lestrade."

———————

Back at our digs in Baker Street, Holmes appeared locked into a process of repairing the grotesque mask to its former splendour. By gumming together the torn shreds of mashed, pulpy material and touching up here and there with water colours, we were able to gaze upon the fierce visage of the object by the sunlight pouring in through the bay window.

"Interesting," said I. "No doubt it once belonged to an island race of cannibal warriors. The bulging eyes bore into you and the snarling mouth speaks of the cooking pot." I folded over the page of my newspaper. "I wonder if old Glenny met his end as part of a ritual slaughter, the plant hunter the victim of a primitive tribe of headsmen?"

"Here in London?" chuckled my companion. "Really, my dear boy, that is a supposition taken too far. Yet, I concede you may be correct to say that a ritual of some kind was involved."

"I have seen similar masks at Horniman Museum," I remarked. "From the islands of Penang, else Indonesia."

"I prefer to conjecture it was once resident in Bali. What purpose it served, whether ceremonial or simply a decorative character in Balinese mythology, I have no idea. Anything of interest in The Telegraph, Watson? I've so far had little opportunity to peruse the morning editions. Where on earth is Mrs Hudson with that pot of coffee?"

"Our lady help is still fuming," said I, browsing through the newspaper. "I fear she shall cook us an inedible supper tonight and be slow to answer your summons. Lestrade knocking her up at half past four has annoyed her. Ah, I see we have an afternoon of entertainment ahead of us at least."

"Really, where's that, then?" asked my companion, putting away his gum brush and pot.

"It says here on page nine,' At two of the clock, an exhibition of the Tuk Tuk Wan, along with its golden portable ancestral spirit house at the Langham Hotel. For an afternoon only in the presence of the raja of Gianlong, the ruler of one of the oldest kingdoms in Bali'. An event open to the general public and free of charge."

"Whether the raja shall be able to escape Dutch colonial rule and a war is doubtful," said Holmes.

"Political unrest means uncertain times lie ahead for him and his subjects."

"Perhaps the raja could reveal more about this mask," said I, lighting a cigar while my companion read the newspaper, taking in every detail of the article.

"The Tuk Tuk Wan is a compelling enough reason to venture forth to the Langham Hotel this afternoon, Watson."

"Indeed."

"According to this short paragraph, the Tuk Tuk Wan is one of the most precious and revered temple effigies in Bali, pre-dating Hindu times. We are in for a visual treat, dear fellow."

"And no entrance fee to pay, which suits my pocket agreeably," I laughed.

"The Balinese treasure also provides us with a clear enough motive for why the plant hunter, Cuthbert Glenny, was murdered and left for the carrion crows to devour at Kew."

At Langham Hotel, the foyer was crowded. A large room had been specially set aside for the exhibition of Balinese culture. After gazing upon various pottery, kites, basket-ware and bamboo furniture, we lined up in an orderly queue to pay our respects to the raja of Gianlong, who was hosting the event.

A completely westernised individual, handsome and dusky of features, he wore the finest clothes Savile Row could offer, shoes by John Lobb, diamond tie clip, pocket watch and fob by Cartier. His noble fingers glittered with precious gems, and a sweetly perfumed garland had been hung round his neck by a liveried servant.

Although fluent in English, he sometimes spoke briefly in Balinese. 'Roko-Roko' he would say when requiring a cigarette. To me, he was both charming and a gentleman of exquisite manners and breeding. He shook me warmly by the hand. My friend, meanwhile, managed to make the serene raja visibly flinch.

"The funerary rites of Bali interest me greatly, your Majesty. I wonder if you could explain how the experienced botanist and plant hunter, Cuthbert Glenny, ended up in a tree at Kew ... murdered?"

"Are you perchance the police?"

"I am a consulting detective, and this is my companion, Dr Watson. I am neither here to apportion blame, or act on behalf of the official Metropolitan force, merely acutely interested to learn more about the plant hunter's death and the peculiar tree burial which I myself witnessed this morning at the botanical gardens in Kew."

The raja, much to his credit, was both frank and to the point.

"Glenny was not all he appeared to be."

"The Tuk Tuk Wan -he stole it, didn't he?"

"Indeed, from my principality in Bali. But listen, Mr Holmes, I cannot speak here. Await the unveiling and afterwards accompany my entourage up to my suite on the top floor. You have my assurance both of you will be made most welcome. I have nothing to hide and am certainly no common criminal capable of murder, as you infer."

We had not long to wait for the unveiling. At a signal from the raja, a traditional silk cloth was drawn aside. For the first time, the British public could gaze upon the notable golden effigy of the Tuk Tuk Wan. One could not help but be impressed by the bejewelled, ugly, toad-like demon squatting on its haunches, a long, spiky tongue dangling from its broad gash of a mouth, the writhing bodies of sacrificial natives being stamped beneath its enormous webbed claws.

"A guardian statue," the raja commented wryly." A talisman of extraordinary power. A sacred effigy that for centuries was guarded by ferocious, man-eating tigers prowling the temple grounds beyond the walls of my palace. But fear not, my dear British guests, although ugly as sin, he is but a rice field toad. Oh, he is so very, very lucky and I am sure he will bestow good fortune on you all."

For our audience with the raja of Gianlong, we were ushered into a small anteroom, being naturally denied access to his personal apartments where his queen and other wives resided privately.

"Dear me, where to start." He shrugged, offering us each an Egyptian cigarette while his valet poured tea. "Cuthbert was a ripping good fellow, absolutely charming and a wonderful and most attentive guest when he stayed with us at Puri Gianlong. I still retain his gifts, intricate drawings of rare plants and orchids, a personal notebook of his travels in Asia Minor, a number of photographs. Such a nice, companionable fellow. I trust him, you see. We were both educated at Eton and Cambridge, and I am myself an amateur botanist. We were of roughly the same age and outlook, the obvious difference being I am blessed with wealth beyond avarice and am ruler of a kingdom with a responsibility to my subjects, many of whom, incidentally, would gladly sacrifice themselves for me should the need arise. I was thrilled when Glemny first wrote to my secretary explaining that he would be visiting Bali in search of rare orchids and would I perhaps like to accompany him on field trips to the temples of Bedulu and Makam Jayaprana."

"Forgive me, your Majesty, but to cut to the chase, am I right in thinking Glenny was not only a plant hunter, but a tenacious hunter of precious artefacts which he hoped to sell for financial gain?"

"How profoundly perceptive of you, Mr Holmes. I'll be generous: maybe he was hard up, needed money to bolster his forthcoming marriage, or on a childish whim he decided to double-cross me and steal the effigy. It matters not. What does matter is that I am, at heart, a botanist, a gardener, a lover of nature, you see. I felt so damn betrayed. My consort, Queen Bhumi, will tell you I am 'an obsessive' and spend much time improving, replanting, nurturing flowers - reinventing, if you will, the paradise I inherited from my father. My life, however, is not without problems. I have the Dutch to contend with and political tensions run high. I may yet have to raise an army to stave off the European aggressor. The problem with Cuthbert Glenny was that he crossed a line and stepped into dangerous waters from which even I could not save him. Listen, gentlemen, despite ruling an old principality, I am myself a modern man well aware of all the latest telegraphic devices, the ebb and flow of the financial markets in London and New York, and so are my closest advisors, my inner court.

My dear father insisted both his future heir, and those closest to him, should be up to date with all the latest developments in the industrial world. Glenny' s huge mistake was to gaze upon my ancient palace and the temple grounds, pass through our villages with their shrines and bamboo huts and regard our culture as quaintly primitive - conveniently backward, if you prefer."

"And pray, when did you learn of the Tuk Tuk Wan's disappearance, your Majesty?"

"Over lunch. Cuthbert was supposedly gone to Karangasam in search of rare plants. One of the monks came to me and told me the ancestral spirit house, the portable garden casket, had been simply unlocked, the temple effigy removed, the key replaced on its hook. I knew who the culprit was, of course."

"No palace guards, no security," said I, incredulously.

"Up till now, there was no need," the raja answered tersely. "Such is the mysterious hold of the Tuk Tuk Wan over my subjects that none should dare gaze upon it without permission, let alone steal it. We are not normally a race of people who go around in a state of suspicion at every turn. Neither are we stupid."

"So, from that very moment you learnt of the robbery, his fate was sealed."

"I had no choice, I was forced to act quickly and decisively. A magnificent deception was required. Both my advisors and I were certain Glenny was headed for England. After all, his marriage to Miss Violet Dunnwiddy was not far into the future. It was imperative we got there ahead of him, firstly to reclaim the Tuk Tuk Wan, secondly to punish the' perpetrator of this heinous crime. A meeting of our council was convened, a number of proposals put forward. It was decided to form a delegation and visit London. We informed the British government by wire that our intention was wholly peaceful and that we should like to launch an exhibition of Balinese culture free of charge to the public, to which your Foreign Office readily agreed.

"By now, we had learnt the plant hunter was aboard a slow-moving cargo steam packet bound for Southampton. It would take ages to reach port. By dusk, my delegation and I were on board one of the fastest ocean-going liners in existence. For a vast, unprecedented sum, I had caused a White Star Line vessel to be diverted in mid-ocean to rendezvous at Lombok. Now we were set fair for England; a swift and luxurious voyage ensued.

"However, that same night, Queen Bhumi, asleep beside me in my berth, I dreamt of the golden Tuk Tuk Wan. The revolting toad seemed to be alive, smiling benignly as blood gushed from its broad mouth and poured down its enormous tongue. It was stamping its feet excitedly.

"I awoke sweating, feeling profoundly apprehen-sive, but of course my consort assured me that all was well, for since the last century, at least, despite its ugli-ness, the demonic toad has in our land become syn-onymous with good luck, so I learnt not to worry and trust our enterprise should prove successful, which it was."

"So, at Southampton your people were able to intercept Glenny?" asked Holmes, lighting another cigarette.

"Outside the customs shed. He was carrying a large, cumbersome carpet bag, the silly, stupid fool. A carpet bag, I ask you!"

"How was he killed - strangled? Stabbed?"

"I do not care how he was killed, Mr Holmes, and neither should you, Dr Watson. It's done, he was basically a crook. The temple elders afforded him the greatest dignity. Monks performed the rites of a tree burial at Kew, his body nobly raised to the skies to be devoured by carrion crows, his spirit set free from the cycle of birth and rebirth. They took into account that part of his life which had been fruitful and studious, his interest in fauna, his love of wild orchids. If only he had not become greedy for gold, betraying my trust, the outcome would have been very different."

A View from Pinckney Street

THE YEAR THAT MY COLLEAGUE, Mr Sherlock Holmes, received his honorary degree from Harvard University, bestowed by Harvard President Merle James Conant at the Tercentenary Theatre, found us across the Atlantic bearing up to an incredibly cold New England winter in Boston. I recall we had already visited Cambridge (Massachusetts) taken round by a Master of Lowell House, seeing for ourselves the pines of Harvard Yard, Wadsworth House, University Hall, the Lamont Library, Blaschka' s glass flowers and plants in the Agassiz Museum, and many striking educational buildings besides.

In the meantime, back at our hotel, the city of Boston came calling in the form of Moreton T. Rockford, the chairman of the immensely prestigious banking firm Rockford Associates, who, for an unprecedented fee, settled us in at a smart little red-brick town house up Beacon Hill, requested Holmes spend some time investigating a fraud, most of which involved sifting through a stash of confidential papers and a box file of accounts invoices entrusted to him and did not require his presence on a daily basis at the bank. Identifying a forged document served, at least, to occupy his clever brain and stave off black moods, and with a New England winter in progress we were housebound, for the most part, anyhow.

Lounging in my rocking chair, a cleverly knocked-together piece of Shaker furniture, I was in two minds about whether to pour myself a second mug of coffee from the enamel pot resting on the wood burner. My friend, I observed, entirely engrossed, puffing on his briar-root pipe, was stooped resolutely over a sheaf of papers with his magnifying lens, spreading out the documents that lent meaning to this bank fraud business upon the smooth top of the antique French-polished table.

I gazed out of the purple glazed window, seeing the occasional muffled-up pedestrian clinging to the rail, making their way precariously down the snowy hill. A very sleek and nifty looking sleigh with tinkling bells, a' cutter' I believe they are called locally in New England, whooshed past. Taking in this wintry scene, I was moreover intrigued to observe a bright-faced, rosy-cheeked young lad towing a small timber toboggan upon which were placed a neat stack of books.

He appeared to be heading directly for our house, thus I hastened along the hall and, upon opening the front door, took a deep draught of Boston's wintry, freezing cold air. It had snowed earlier, and a white drift piled high on the step.

"You them Londoners from Baker Street?" The boy spoke with a youthful gaiety.

"We are," I answered.

"Mr Sherwood Holmes lives 'ere, don't 'e?"

"Sherlock, sonny, Sherlock Holmes, but indeed he does, No.64."

"You Mr Shylock?"

"No, but I'll willingly pass on a message."

The boy pushed some gummy substance he was chewing to one side of his cheek before answering.

"Say, Mister - tell him an old guy called Hedonist Carr bin asking for him down at the Athenaeum Library. Wants to see 'im, says it's real important - values your time, an' all."

"The 'Master of the Macabre' - *that* Hedonist Carr?" said I incredulously, my chest bursting with a rush of excitement at the mere mention of the author's name.

"Yep, the same. Why, you read his books? I like ' em lots, but Ma detests every word. She'd ban 'em, says reading the likes of Poe and Carr'll turn me into an axe murderer 'fore time I git to thirteen. Says I'll carve up my own grandmother an' bury her beneath the stoop."

"I'm sure she's being playfully facetious," I laughed, "exaggerating somewhat." Ruffling his hair, I pressed a shiny new dime into the palm of his woollen mitten. "We'll get down to the Athenaeum right away."

"Library looks onto the granary burying ground -can't miss it."

"And grand good luck with your reading endeavours," I called out after him as the boy, looking very pleased with himself, went on his way, dragging that toboggan of his with its runners scraping along the walkway.

The New England author Hedonist Carr, I should explain, at that time outsold Poe, Harriet Beecher Stowe, Mark Twain, Nathaniel Hawthorne and Melville by many millions with what critics on both sides of the Atlantic were wont to describe variously as novels of 'execrable garbage', 'macabre to the extreme', 'horribly good' and 'blood-soaked and grisly enough for the charnel house', which goaded the general public, myself included, to go out and purchase his books that I personally found always first-rate and entertaining. It turned out he resided in Louisburg Square where there is an oval-shaped iron fenced little garden bearing a stone-carved figure of Columbus in its midst, although I only found this out later. But I digress.

At first, loath to quit his, I am certain, very able and exhaustive search for a forged document, my companion, I suspect welcoming a less arduous diversion, at length gathered his stout fur-collard coat, deerstalker, galoshes and silver-topped cane and together we set off downhill.

————————

We took the trolley-car to the front of Park Street church and walked briskly from there, fresh flurries of snow and a sharp wind making it feel all the colder.

Darting through the doors of the Athenaeum Library, we made our tentative approach to the curved rosewood desk behind which presided a formidable, bespectacled lady librarian, no doubt an academic, wearing formal grey skirt and starched white blouse, eyeing us with the proper invested authority of a privately run institution founded by a number of subscribers in 1807. She bade us come hither.

"Can I help, gentlemen? Which floor do you require? The George Washington Exhibition is in the Trustees Room on the fourth. Were you specially invited by Dr Willard Cogswell? A number of guests have already gone up," said she, politely.

"No," I whispered in respectful tones, informing the librarian that a certain local New England author had requested our presence for an interview. She indicated beyond the panelled reading room with its well -ordered books, spotless chairs and desks, long tables and marble busts displayed in wall niches, to a cosy nook where, before a cheery coal fire, we caught our first glimpse of a very plump and friendly-looking gentleman with long, silvery hair, dressed from head to foot in black, who, upon seeing us, walked us over, settling us in a pair of most excellent leather club chairs beside the fire.

"Be seated," said he, his chubby face aglow with good cheer. "I have an entire collection of your case accounts from Lippincott' s monthly magazine bound in brocaded green vellum and I am honoured to make the acquaintance of London's famous consulting detective and his no less worthy biographer."

"It's a pleasure," I answered, gripping the venerable scribe's outstretched lardy hand in mine, close to tears, for in truth, I had, over the years, devoured his many novels of horror and indeed possessed, under my bed, a tatty suitcase stuffed with many worn and much-read yellow-back editions.

"You are familiar, I take it, with 'Old Ed'," he enquired, relighting his corn-cobber with enthusiasm.

"Certainly," Holmes replied with sombre reflection, retrieving his briar-root pipe and sealskin pouch from his coat pocket. "Edgar Allan Poe, you refer to, of course. I've read many of his works. *The Narrative of Arthur Gordon Pym of Nantucket*, his short novella, I found wanting and patchy, but his shorter fiction shows promise. *August Dupin* has some merit, I suppose."

"Merit! Why, that little guy Poe practically invented the fictional detective. I knew him, of course. A hopeless sot - any time I saw him in New York he was invariably drunk. Poe was a ferocious critic, you know, and never possessed a kindly or helpful word for any of my early novels. But his genius will one day be recognised, although he earnt little money from his writing when alive, and me a mere scribbler gets by very nicely."

"You have the popular touch, Mr Carr," said I. "That's a rare enough gift in itself."

I was, I recall at the time, grinning like a besotted puppy dog.

Over a lifetime's career, Carr must have become almost blase about receiving similar praise and adulation, for in no time, he seemed distracted and, even while I was eagerly waxing lyrical about his books, was looking straight past me. In any event, I twisted round and there was a dormer window with a view into the main square. I observed a glass-sided hearse trotting through the churned-up snow while in the other direction, on more compounded substance, a convoy of sleighs drawn by single nags swished across the square, bells jangling.

"Seems to me," the writer muttered, peering inquisitively over my shoulder, "that damn undertaker, Kraal, is our hometown Rasputin. How the women flock round him, charisma, charm, whatever you label such manly effervescence, he sure possesses that quality - an' him with that city funeral parlour and handling corpses day 'n' night!"

"Quite," said Holmes firmly. "Mr Carr, might I enquire as to why exactly you wished to ... "

Barely were these words spoken by my companion than the old fellow's jowls quivered and a quantity of pipe ash spilled down his black waistcoat. Carr, with a look of admonition, stumped his ivory-handled cane thrice upon the bare, varnished floorboards and boomed in a loud, commanding voice, "Say, call me Hedonist - all my friends do, please, gentlemen. You English are too damned formal. Let's cut Her Majesty the Queen Vic's airs and graces for now, shall we?"

"Very well," answered Holmes good-naturedly. "Hedonist, why did you request this interview, given that Watson here is an enthusiastic consumer of those shilling shocker novels of yours back home and will shortly demand an autograph?"

"Most kind. Well, Sherlock, and you too, Doc - I guess I should strike to the quick. Truth is, I could use some of your expertise, your overview, if you will. There's a new book I'm planning, non-fiction, an exposé, of sorts. Mark you, I've had my suspicions for a long while, oh yes, and Ill not be intimated, nor sidelined. So help me, I'll make sure justice is done. It's all here in my head, see, clear as day, nothing committed to paper as yet, you understand - safer that way. I'll get to the finer details presently, but for now... "

Striking a match and lighting his pipe, Holmes became visibly agitated. "I must caution such labours, for they often have a habit of backfiring. For instance, if you be proved mistaken, you open yourself to lengthy and painful litigation. If you slander someone, Mr Carr, you can be sued in a court of law for every cent you possess. Your reputation, your comfortable author's existence here in Boston, all threatened, your fortune much diminished by fearsome legal expenses. Is it, I put to you at your time of life, this noble quest to accomplish a somewhat precarious literary endeavour more often as not fuelled by some petty grudge, envy, else a misguided sense of moral purpose, really worth it?"

"Most ably put, Sherlock, and I thank you for your considered apprehensions. However, I did not embark upon this mission of expose lightly. I have a top publisher's legal team in New York whose job is to keep me out of trouble and my long-time agent, Owen Mallet, is the best. I say to you gentlemen yet again, that despite risk, precuniary or otherwise, justice will be done. My one aim all along has been to bring this sonofabitch to ... "

At the time, concerning myself filling my pipe with Auld Mayflower tobacco, whilst simultaneously listening to Carr's pleasantly spoken New England burr, I was all of a sudden aware of a long, drawn out sigh - a wheezing expulsion of air from the lung sacs, and, glancing up, was in time to witness the elderly shocker writer topple forward in his chair.

By his collapsed condition, and the lack of response when my colleague, Mr Sherlock Holmes, shook the old fellow firmly by the shoulders, shouting for a nearby attendant to fetch a glass of brandy that instant, I was in no hesitation judging him to have breathed his last.

If readers imagine that this sudden death of a notable writer was deemed to be in any way remotely suspicious, they will, alas, like Sherlock Holmes himself, be bitterly disappointed.

As a retired physician, I was first to examine the author's motionless figure slumped before the library fire and can vouch a deceased heart and the ravages of old age_ responsible for his death - simple as that - and this prognosis was backed up by the medical examiner, Hank Streeter, who later informed us that Hedonist Carr had, for some time, been suffering from a faulty heart valve.

However, the timing of the death was, for us at least, frustrating, for I and my illustrious colleague were left with no clue as to whom exactly the writer intended to expose, nor, either, the nature of criminal intent involved. Being but visitors to Boston, and knowing few people in the capital, was not exactly helpful either.

―――――

We attended the author's funeral some days later, and whilst the glass-sided hearse slowly proceeded from snowbound Louisburg Square, followed by a sedate line of mourning coaches, pausing at the steepled church and universalist meeting house before heading up the hill to the cemetery, it was obvious that Hedonist Carr, 'the Master of the Macabre', was held in great esteem by members of the public, for the route was lined by a fair number of mourners.

Thus, on that exposed hill, awaiting its next assiduous topping of snow, we observed, whilst Thomas Kraal stood proud as Attica overseeing the removal of the large, hefty coffin from the rear of the hearse by his assistants, a late carriage draw up at the gates. It came to a halt and remained poised, as it were, but no one stepped down, nor could any hint of a visage be seen at the window, so it seemed to me this particularly reticent mourner chose to witness the interment discreetly from a distance, having no desire to join the rest of us crowding round the graveside.

But to elaborate, let me recall a queer incident that occurred halfway through prayers. We mourners stood huddled together, shivering as a group, whereupon a tall, elegantly turned-out lady, her face concealed by a veil, rushed amongst us and attempted to ferociously seize the arm of the undertaker, Thomas Kraal, who quickly stood back, avoiding her grasping hand.

"My fault, all my fault," she cried at him bitterly. "But you, you in whom I put my whole faith. You, sir, have left me misguided, piteously adrift. Oh, what have I done but got what I deserved - this terror unending!"

Alas, the sloping, uneven ground caused one of the heels of her dainty calfskin boots to skew awkwardly, as with arms flailing, she nearly ended up toppling into the yawning mouth of the recently excavated grave, but was prevented from so doing by a rush of gallants, that is quick-witted gentlemen, Nathaniel Hawthorne's grown son Julian amongst them, who I had been informed travelled down from Concord to attend, and it was they who managed to subdue this poor, distressed creature, hurrying her away across the white-carpeted landscape of partly-sunken and crookedly-angled headstones to that same mysterious carriage we noted earlier, waiting further down.

Holmes and myself, I hasten to add, were none the wiser as we first headed back down the hill as to the identity of the veiled lady, and it must be said, the undertaker, Thomas Kraal, managed admirably to keep his composure for the remainder of the burial ceremony, apparently unruffled, and maintaining, outwardly at least, an appearance of calm and affability.

Then came some enlightenment from the officiating minister, the Reverend Hartford, who sat in the same carriage as we, although rather pasty-faced and sickly looking, a most affable and talkative individual.

"You know, gentlemen," he remarked, taking a generous pinch of snuff, "I've seen, over the past month, the emergence of an increasing number of veiled ladies who attend church, just for the Sunday, and say nothing to anyone, nor mix with my flock after service. I'd dread to think we have a secret mediumistic society in our midst. I mean, London's got the bug aint' it? Levitation, table rapping, the planchette, all the rage, I guess; but here in Boston, I pray not."

"You were chatting with Hawthorne's son earlier. His father, Nathaniel, I recall wrote a novel entitled *The Blithedale Romance* which made much mention of a veiled lady," said I.

"I never read it myself, Dr Watson," remarked the minister languidly, peering out of the carriage window.

"He tended to rather play up his Salem ancestry and makes much mention of witchcraft in his novels and shorter works, of which I disapprove."

"By the by," asked my colleague, pulling a rug further over his long legs, "the veiled lady back at the cemetery, the one who tried to accost Thomas Kraal - any idea who she is?"

The minister stroked his cleft chin thoughtfully. "Nancy Vandergaard, a wealthy Bostonian heiress."

"Resident in a sanatorium, perhaps?"

"Great heavens, I should hope not! Her summer residence is one of the most exclusive mansions in Bellvue Avenue, Newport, and she keeps a house in Boston, of course, and a host of secretaries and servants besides."

"Do you, perchance, have any inkling as to the reason for her rage?"

"My guess is as good as yours, Mr Holmes -a rival for her misplaced affections, a falling-out, some silly carrying-on -women do get so intense, so passionate over a man they wish to ensnare, to possess utterly. I thank the Lord I am a committed bachelor."

My colleague laughed, but his beady eyes either

side of that great beaky nose were sly and calculating.

"Given that Thomas Kraal has a reputation as a Lothario, something of a ladies' man, yet I cannot countenance a well-heeled Bostonian heiress involved in a tawdry affair with the owner of a funeral parlour. Although feasible, an assignation seems to me unlikely," he sighed. "I'd wager the cause of her passionate outburst was entirely unrelated. I think we can discount any romantic entanglement, but she had it in for him alright, that much was clear!"

At half past six of the following evening, beneath the steady glow emitted from the ornate lantern bracketed outside our little red brick abode, a cutter sleigh drew up at Pinckney Street and I beheld from the front window a tall, exquisitely attired lady drop aside her whip, stepping nimbly down into the crisp snow and, after patting the pony, reassuring the beast, made haste across the walkway to our front door.

She wore a fashionable and very exclusive white mink coat and fur hat and, despite her veil, strode with considerable confidence, whereupon I opened the door to our surprise visitor.

"Mr Sherlock Holmes, the London consulting detective?"

"I am Dr Watson, but pray allow me to take your winter furs, my dear. Step this way. Holmes is presently racking his brains concerning a banking scam and will, I am sure, welcome lighter diversion."

I, of course, welcomed this feminine diversion also. Her perfume, a divine fragrance, wafted in her wake about the front hall and, despite the covering veil, I sensed a warm and charming personality lay concealed beneath, being thus doubly rewarded when, once ensconced in our cosily lamp-lit parlour with its contrasting mix of Shaker and eighteenth-century French antique furnishings, she gracefully removed her veil and we were privileged to gaze upon her strikingly handsome features. My heart raced contemplating this blonde Bostonian beauty, and as I showed her to the cushioned divan she offered me a considered look, an earnest appraisal as to whether perhaps I could be entirely trusted.

"Miss Vandergaard, welcome," said Holmes kindly. "A glass of sherry, although I hear you eminently fashionable young ladies of Boston and Rhode Island prefer a 'gin sling', else bourbon on the rocks."

"Nothing for me, thank you, Mr Holmes. Myself, I prefer not to touch the stuff."

"Your wearing the veil adds a touch of flair - you become a woman of mystery."

Miss Vandergaard gave a timid smile.

"I wear this veil out of respect for the late and much-lamented writer Hedonist Carr; a personage, I confess, who loyally, and in confidence, tendered me advice some time past which I alas failed abysmally to heed, and have, as a consequence, lived to pay a large price. It was his funeral only recently after all, a decent period of mourning is surely in order -where is the mystery in that?"

"Forgive me, I shall proceed to lighten our discourse somewhat by begging you a trifling favour."

"Go ahead," she laughed, sensing my companion's good humour.

"Those wonderfully beguiling ruby earrings you wear, might I closer inspect them? The settings appear very 'Regency' and stately."

"The earrings were bequeathed me by my late mother. They are my favourites. Old English Cheapside silver and gemstones, to be sure."

"My companion gently settled himself down on the divan beside Miss Vandergaard, allowing for her to tuck strands of blonde hair behind one ear. She was flattered, pleased with the attention. Pleased, that is, until her womanly intuition became suddenly aware that her entire face was being meticulously appraised, which naturally unsettled her.

Sensing he had been over intrusive, Holmes took out his silver case and offered round cigarettes. I lit hers with a vesta.

"Might I enquire the actual reason you chose to visit us this evening, Miss Vandergaard? As a consulting detective, if it is in my power to assist you in any way I will do so. My talents are at your disposal. Your impromptu visit concerns Thomas Kraal, I take it."

The woman's eyes appeared bewildered, pleading. She shuddered.

"Him, yes, no. Oh, I meant to have such a heart to heart with you. I'd planned such a pow-wow in my head, you see, gentlemen, but now I'm actually here, I would fain tell you the truth but cannot."

"You argued, or at least you appeared to wish to confront the undertaker about some galling issue. Does it concern payment of large sums of money? Are you, perchance, being blackmailed? For that is, I confess, my own assumption. Miss Vandergaard, it is requisite that you give me some indication of your part in the affair."

"Him., yes, yes -but no, not blackmail, nothing like that. Pardon me, Mr Holmes, but I have to leave. I came here honestly hoping to enlighten you as to my predicament, but it's no use. I must go at once. Forgive me -my fault, all my wretched fault."

She wrung her hands. So pitiful to behold this attractive Bostonian heiress seize her veil and replace it, her countenance ravaged by some inner turmoil of conscience.

I did my utmost to pacify our visitor, but to no avail. She allowed me, at least, to enfold her in voluptuous white furs and, thanking me profusely, Miss Vandergaard rushed into wintry Pinckney Street to board her waiting sleigh. I and my companion could hear the harness bells jangling way down the hill.

"Well," said I, slumping in my rocker, nursing a stiff whisky. "That's about as useless a half hour as we've ever spent, old man. If only she'd confided in us more, trusted us."

"On the contrary. Miss Vandergaard, quite unwittingly it so happens, provided me with a host of excellent data. But firstly, Watson, consider this old copy of the *Atlantic Monthly*. Let's see what you make of the picture spread. I ringed a particular photograph in red ink."

Leaning forward, I snatched the publication and gave it the greatest scrutiny. The article in question was self-explanatory, due to the pictures and captions. *'Miss Nancy Vandergaard, along with her pug dogs, Winnie, Bess and Jerome, is seen showing the palatial interior of her mansion at 243 Bellevue Avenue in Newport, designed by architect Standford White.'*

"Look here, Holmes," said I. "There has clearly been an editorial error. The woman shown in this photograph is surely the mother. Our pretty visitor tonight is, I should say, six and twenty. The lady shown here, although similar of feature, must be five and forty."

"My dear Watson," said my erstwhile colleague, lighting a cigarette with the benevolent air of a patient teacher persevering with a rather dim-witted pupil. "Do you recall my examining those earrings of hers rather closely?"

"I do. Your remarkable, if uncharacteristic, intimacy, the nearness of your face to hers, caused her certain consternation, her breathing quickened, I noticed that."

"Excellent! Your observation does you great credit, although you saw none of the faint scarring, I take it. Of course you didn't."

"What I saw, my dear Holmes, and who amongst us men could forget, was a very pretty face."

"Did it not strike you that her lips, particularly the lower, protruded somewhat, appeared over-inflated?"

"Sensuous and pouting is the more proper description," I laughed. "Why do you analyse so?"

"The loose folds of skin about the throat had been diminished. Did that allure you also?"

"What on earth are you driving at?"

Leaning back in his chair, Holmes appeared very grave and thoughtful. Staring a while at the rumbling wood stove, he lit yet another cigarette.

"So, it has come to this," he reflected dolefully. "Now it appears they can embalm one before you're even dead. At least the Egyptians allowed a decent interval. I can hardly credit such audacity."

"I'm not quite with you, old chap."

"Let us return to the earrings," said he, seriously. "Under close scrutiny, it became clear to me that the frontal part of her head, that is from forehead to chin, had been subtly restructured. Just above the hairline, I was astounded to see the skin stretched upward to allow for a smoother, younger appearance, reducing the lines of natural ageing. I observed very faint, barely discernible scars where stitching had been applied. For instance, beneath the chin and pertaining to the throat, the pouches beneath her eyes so evident, so normal at her time of life, somehow lessened. My dear boy, you only have to consult the periodical to witness the ordinary ageing process to which we are all, incidentally, beholden. The actual age of Nancy Vandergaard, the lady we saw here tonight, is indeed five and forty if a day."

"But that set-to on the hill at the funeral," said I. "I mean, from what you infer, I abhor the undertaker's back-room practice, yet clearly she has nothing to complain about, her countenance is duly enhanced. She looks younger than her years." I gulped the remainder of my whisky. "All this self-loathing, wringing of hands; what in the Lord's name has got into her?"

"By Jove, Watson, it's a case of crushed vanity, dear boy - dashed hopes. One can but conjecture that she learnt fairly recently from another wiser, more perceptive party, that her new enhanced looks are medically flawed and fast waning, which had never been the initial idea. This is what causes the turmoil, this dichotomy to race within her breast, and yet she cannot adequately find it within herself to condemn the deceitful perpetrator, the one who promised a safe and sure procedure. That is why, of course, she visited us this evening, I'll warrant. Has the penny not dropped yet, Watson? That wise informant I mention is Hedonist Carr. The villain of the piece he wished to expose in his proposed book being none other save Thomas Kraal for malpractice. The decent thing for us to do now is, to the best of our ability, finish off, to conclude that which the shocker and latter-day writer of conscience actually intended. Thus tonight, under cover of darkness, we perform a necessary break-in. Pour us another glass of that first-rate Bourbon, dear boy, and pass over the pouch of Auld Mayflower tobacco you've been hogging

———

Later that night, wrapped up fitfully, but by no means impervious to dipping temperatures, Holmes and I set out on our quest. Beside the houses was an iron railing, useful for us inhabitants to hold onto when going up or down the hill in slippery conditions, employed also for tethering horses, and we clung to this like grim death. It was an icy night and we eventually crossed to the edge of the embankment at the bottom of the hill, upon the other side of which the Charles River flowed. The main road was deserted; no one was abroad, neither Hackney coach, sleighs or trolley-car in evidence, and we headed more stealthily into the city without meeting a soul. A Boston pictorial guide offered adequate directions, but it was still an hour or so before we reached the funeral parlour premises belonging to Thomas Kraal.

I checked my silver pocket watch. Here we were, about to perform a break-in. My nerves were on edge, Holmes employing his tried and trusted formula for springing the most stubborn lock - the humble yet wholly effective pipe-knife. Bent low to the keyhole, twisting and poking about until the mechanism gave a resounding click, the door creaked open and we crept inside.

By choosing the side entrance round by the stable block we avoided the reception rooms and coffin showroom, preferring to take our chances with the rooms at the back. Presumably coffins were conveyed through this door and slid on rollers into the back of the hearse for funerals.

Cautiously lighting a shaded oil lamp, we moved almost, it felt like, inch by inch between a group of coffins perched on trestles.

"This is the chapel of rest, Watson. Our nocturnal quest takes us, however, toward that thick velvet plush curtain on the far side with the boldly inscribed notice 'PRIVATE - MORTUARY DEPT' above. Be a good fellow and open my cigarette case, will you? Help yourself, yes. Let's light up, it's as damnably chilly in here as outside, I fear."

The curtain was deftly drawn aside; my friend shone the lamp beam about the tiled room. Glinting in the shadowy glow from the light reflected on the shiny surfaces were shelves of stoppered glass medical jars, with which, as a doctor and one time student at Barts, I was well familiar. I confess, the first occasion both of us took fright in that home for the dead was the instant we spied what floated inside these receptacles, for we were confronted by row upon row of pickled, cut-away faces suspended in varying strengths of murky preservative solution. Women, men both old and young, and children thereby whose facial features resembled, at best, deflated India rubber masks, void of eyeballs and teeth.

"Well, don't look so perplexed, dear boy," said Holmes, doing his best to compose himself after the initial shock. "One must expect Kraal learned his craft by initial experimentation. Why, it appears even our writer friend, Hedonist Carr, failed to escape being facially scalped. See here, the fleshy, distinctive features reside in jar No.32 where I'm pointing with my cane."

"These insipid masks," said I, "heretofore severed by his, the mortician's, artful fingers from tissue, means many a body was committed for burial up at the cemetery not whole or entire - a despicable business."

"I concur, and, my dear Watson, we can therefore take immense satisfaction in burning down the premises forthwith. Once we have removed the horses from the stable, that is, and settled them in the far field."

"Burn the place down, Holmes! Are you mad?"

"I have an urgent requirement to see Police Chief Gordon and the District Attorney. What quicker way to bring this business off than a town fire?"

"You'll not burn anything!" answered an angry voice from beyond the velvet plush curtain. "This be my property, raised on my land. You'll be civil enough to move out of my embalming room to where I can see you better, gentlemen."

"The facial remains in the jars accuse you," said I haughtily.

"The faces in the jars greatly helped me learn my trade. As a trespasser, your moral rectitude does you credit, sir, but it struck me early on that my particular funerary line of trade left me uniquely placed to broaden my business interests. I am also aware of the little vanities women be so susceptible to. What harm can there be cutting about stiffs bound to rot under six feet of clay anyhow? However, movin' on - 'why am I here?' you fellas may well ask. Weil, not to tend to the stiffs, that's for sure. I'm here on account of Hal Morgan 'cross the way who, bein' a goodly neighbour of mine, saw a queer light movin' about and sent his son to alert me of criminal mischief. Lucky for some, but not you English, I guess."

"Recalling, no doubt, this great capital's patriotic fervour during the Boston Tea Party, we need to talk, Mr Kraal."

"No time. Why, I've got a pair of cheapskate pine caskets I'd be glad to part with fer free, and once I've shot you both dead, that's where ya'll be layin' fer a long while, fellas."

But while Thomas Kraal concerned himself with our imminent execution, totally distracted, five veiled shapes, by means of the conveniently open side door, entered the gloomy precincts of the Chapel of Rest, gliding amongst the gloating array of trestle coffins with barely a rustle, forming a committed procession. It appeared, under the preternatural ambience of the moon, mayhap a visitation of shades from the hilltop were emboldened to create night time mischief.

Dainty on her feet and purposeful, the first, the leader, a very tall and lithe figure, crept up behind the boorish undertaker.

"You are most kind to offer us one of your cheap coffins, Mr Kraal, but I think a trifle prematurely. I should prefer to wait awhile. I'd rather fancy a lead-lined ... "

My companion, Mr Sherlock Holmes, kept up a mildly sarcastic banter. Barely had Kraal raised his Colt revolver, about to squeeze the trigger and aiming at my chest, I being nearest, my heart counting the seconds I had left to live, when a finely-bladed scalpel lashed through the darkness striking our Mr Kraal above the collar, at his fleshy, exposed neck. The blood spurts following reminded one of a bullring in Malaga, but here at the downtown funeral home more than one conquistador was vying to weaken and subjugate the bull.

The broad-shouldered, squat undertaker had barely a chance to fend off a second vicious assault delivered by another participant, this time from the front. A long-bladed scalpel was thrust through the gelatine-like substance of his left eye, causing Kraal to fall to his knees in an ever-widening pool of blood. Moaning and clutching his face, still more blows reigned down until he lay quite dead, sprawled t amongst the coffins he was so famous for supplying.

Thus, the five veiled ladies--hastily departed, their long skirts and winter fur coats rustling across the floor as they each headed for the stable yard.

Barely had the mysterious ladies left when Holmes thrust a carboy of formaldehyde spirit into my hands and together we began sprinkling preservative all about the place. Whilst I hurried to the stables and proceeded to lead the horses away to the safety of the field, my companion, meanwhile, struck a match and thereby began a chemical blaze of considerable force that quickly took hold. In fact, I recall, by the time we arrived back at our little red brick house in Pinckney Street after walking up the hill, dawn was breaking and morning boating activities beginning on the Charles River.

While I lay comfortably abed in my upstairs room, still I heard quite distinctly the jangling bells of steam fire pumps, no doubt tearing across the city joining other machines converging, else present, at the scene of the, by then surely, utterly destroyed and smouldering remains of the funeral parlour.

The following morning, we awoke later than planned and were eager to discuss the implications of the night before. Outside, it was a sunny blue sky and the snowy outlook reflected whiter than before.

"The affair, I grant you, is a complicated one," admitted Holmes, settling down before the wood stove after he had consumed a hearty breakfast of steak and eggs and about to smoke the first pipe of the day.

I might add, a crucial letter had arrived that same morning from a: Professor T.W. McCord, a lecturer at Harvard Medical School, who had diligently answered a number of points put forward by Holmes in writing regarding radical surgery to the face. I shall not bore the reader here with medical jargon, else long drawn-out anatomical details, but, I hasten to add, it made disturbing reading.

In his view, and Professor McCord had extensive and first-hand experience of battlefield injury, making incisions, stretching facial skin into shape thus reducing ageing lines posed something of a dilemma. Temporarily, the initial surgery would, perhaps, hold up well, but in this age, at least, be only sustainable for six months or so, whereupon the fleshy matter should collapse leaving the face terribly mutilated and deformed. He warned Holmes against any such procedure and thus was plainly spelt out the awful fate awaiting Nancy Vandergaard, of which she must surely have been made aware, and the other wealthy Rhode Island ladies foolhardy enough to place their looks and well-being in the hands of that unscrupulous undertaker, Thomas Kraal.

My colleague, over a pipe full of Auld Mayflower coarse tobacco, which had quite taken our fancy over the past fortnight while staying in Boston, surmised thus: "My dear Watson, it is, of course, most likely these chastened women shall flee to Europe and thus live out their lives cloistered in a sympathetic convent far away from the public gaze."

I objected, finding this stark prediction too depressing. I offered my own more optimistic alternative: "Is it not more likely, Holmes, these New England ladies shall form a commune and buy up an attractive villa in Italy, else a sunny French chateau isolated by an immense tract of land and live secluded in the relative luxury surrounded by devoted servants?"

We agreed to differ, and thereby was brought a fitting conclusion, our efforts to validate the late shocker writer Hedonist Carr's worthy efforts to stamp out this folly of woman's vanity.

Perhaps, in any case, pursuing Thomas Kraal was a trifle more energetic than the rather low-key Boston banking scam, for which a line of altered accounts and a falsified signature were eventually discovered by my dear friend's skilled use of the magnifying lens searching amongst minutiae.

The Haversham Jackdaw

ON NEW YEAR'S DAY, in that bitter winter of 1890, Holmes and myself were walking down Baker Street from the Oxford Street end.

Despite sporadic scatterings of cinders, the pavements of the metropolis were icy and treacherous underfoot. It had started snowing again and there was a fierce northerly wind. Much to our amusement-. for mirth has a warming way about it - an elderly gentleman upon the other side of the street was bracing himself to fend off the swirling sleet with his umbrella when, quite unexpectedly, due to a particularly strong gust, the shaft parted company with the handle!

The poor fellow grimly held on and watched aghast whilst the rest of his brolly rose into the air and floated across the street like a gigantic crow. It came crashing down and proceeded to slide along the icy pavement as though it were on skates.

Holmes, evidently enjoying himself, ran after it, managed to trap the wayward brolly beneath his shoe and energetically stamped upon the thing a couple of times - presumably to kill it.

"Why, thank you, sir," said the gentleman, as he came-puffing across the road to claim his other half.

"You shall have to get it repaired," said I. "There is a place along Wimpole Street - do you know it?"

"I fear I shall have to throw it away, sir," said he, carefully examining the twisted spokes and rent canvas. "But I am nonetheless extremely grateful to your friend here. I should not have fancied being taken to court over the loss of an eye, or worse. By the way, does either of you gentlemen live hereabouts?"

"Yes, we do. Whose place are you after?"

"I am looking for a Mr Sherlock Holmes," he replied. "I've tried at least three addresses so far, all of them up at the metropolitan end, and not managed to find him yet!"

"Then you need look no further," said I, "for by way of coincidence, Mr Sherlock Holmes is the very man who has just rescued your umbrella!"

"Thank God," said he, evidently much relieved. "My name is Reginald Canty, sir, and I am a retired accountant from Surrey."

"Well, Mr Canty," my friend said, adjusting his scarf, "I take it that whatever led you to stray from your hearth on such a brazenly cold morning as this must be of some importance! The number is 221B, by the way."

The snow had started to fall heavily and we scrambled into a cab and followed the main artery of traffic back to our lodgings.

Canty was a likeable enough character. He possessed the dignified, reserved manner of an ex-City man, hardened, and slightly cynical, from decades of commuting. Bright green eyes held you in a steady gaze and a square, determined jaw spoke of a lifetime of responsibility concerning banking procedures and company balance sheets.

Holmes and myself settled back in our armchairs in front of the bright, cheery fire and listened with considerable interest as Canty explained why he had troubled to commute from Haversham to seek out the advice of my colleague.

"There has been a New Year's Eve burglary, Mr Holmes," said he. "In fact, I regret to say, several of them!"

"Hum, and you were one of the casualties, I take it?"

"That is correct," he replied, and worse, I have no inkling how the thief broke into my house, and still less how he actually managed to escape. The matter does not simply rest there, however, for this morning I received a summons from my neighbour, Philip Lamb, a bank manager, and discovered, to my surprise, that his own house had been burgled and he, in turn, had been informed that the house opposite, belonging to Stanley Rogers, a broker, had received a dose of the same!"

"And, pray, exactly what was stolen?"

"Jewellery, sir. My wife lost her diamond tiara, a ruby necklace and several rings. Although, strangely enough, none of my own personal effects were touched, and this proved to be the case with Lamb and Rogers."

"Did you inform the police about the theft?"

"I did not wish to have my name, or that of my wife, manufactured in print and used to enliven innumerable headlines and sell newspapers. Rogers and Lamb felt likewise. The matter has not been discussed outside our circle. We celebrated the New Year and our servants joined us at midnight to partake of the customary toast. At well past one, my wife decided to go upstairs to bed. I was about to join her, but thought it prudent to remind Matthews, a sincere and obliging fellow and altogether one of the most sensible domestics we have ever employed, that one of the windows in the conservatory required battening. Shortly after, my wife gave out the most fearful scream."

"And where did your wife normally keep her jewellery?"

"In a Chippendale cabinet beside her dressing table."

"And it was unlocked?"

"Certainly! I mean, a lady does not expect to have her boudoir suddenly broken into! Although it was still bitterly cold, I remember no snow had fallen since the previous afternoon, thus, after comforting my wife and leaving a servant with her, I decided to take Matthews, together with the dogs and a lantern, and search every inch of my property. I was determined that if the thief had left behind any tell-tale evidence of his night's work, I should be the first to discover it! Outside, the cylindrical ridge of snow running along the length of the stone walling bordering my garden remained unbroken. I therefore surmised that no one had attempted to climb over it."

"How perceptive of you!" remarked my colleague, with a twinkle in his eyes, smoking his pipe and glancing out at the sleet pattering against the windowpane.

"Oh, I have a weakness for crime novels and the like, Mr Holmes, and thought I might be able to put the knowledge I had gleaned to practical use."

"Ha! Please don't keep us in suspense, Mr Canty. Perhaps you could tell us about the prints you discovered on the lawn."

"Well, I was about to get to that," said the retired accountant, becoming overtly puffed up, unaware of my companion's humorous turn of mind and, no doubt, imagining he was about to follow in the steps of Poe and produce some masterly oracle of detection.

The lawn was covered in snow to a depth of, I should say, about a foot. All I could discern from its frozen surface were the prints of my dogs and various species of bird. The moonlit path seemed to be very much the same as I remembered it the evening before.

"Matthews, I think, visited the bird table on a few occasions. No one else, apart from the dogs, had ventured across it for days. I then turned to face the house and perceived the window ledges had not been trampled on, if a ladder had been used, I could find no sign of one - anywhere. We possess a long ladder with two stages of rungs, and yet nobody had been near it."

"My dear Watson, from what Mr Canty has told us so far, this portends to be a most singular case. We have three houses, each in close proximity to the other. Granted, the New Year festivities allow a considerable leeway for the burglar. However, you mentioned you keep dogs, Mr Canty?"

"Indeed, we all do," he said with some surprise. "My spaniel barks at the slightest provocation, and Lizzie, the Scotch terrier, although inclined to be of a more placid temperament, will join in whenever the opportunity arises. Stanley Rogers keeps a black Labrador; Lamb, a collie!"

"Haversham's in Surrey, isn't it?" said Holmes. "Do many trains run there on New Year's Day?"

"A normal service. Trains leave Victoria on the half-hour every hour, passing through Croydon. However, bad weather might have affected the times, you know, frozen points, else a portion of line blocked by snow."

"Then I suggest we forfeit the excellent wild duck Mrs Hudson was preparing for lunch, Watson, and take a cab straightaway to Victoria."

We arrived at Haversham at just past two. The train was late, for the signals were working very badly and there were intermittent delays along the line. Canty lived in a pleasant wooded cul-de-sac on the outskirts of Haversham, not far from Deacons Common and the Swan Inn. The area was fairly well-to-do, with most properties belonging to retired City accountants, stockbrokers and the like.

In pointing out the houses belonging to Philip Lamb and his neighbour, Stanley Rogers, Canty made it clear that each had been designed by the quirky Scandinavian architect, Svenson, and this accounted for the peculiar mixture of styles - best described as a combination of 'European' and British 'medieval'. For instance, the front of Canty' s residence was built like an Alpine hunting lodge, with a round Norman turret at either end, whereas to confuse matters, the back incorporated the traditional Tudor facade of rosy brickwork, many timbers and latticed windows. This was not so bizarre to the Englishman's eye as it might at first appear, for the bad weather enhanced the aspect of these dwellings wonderfully, and in this landscape one could quite easily have been about to test the slopes of the Tyrol, or encounter a herdsman with his reindeer!

We were greeted beneath the snow-covered porch by Mrs Canty and her two dogs, and shown into a large, airy drawing room, comfortably furnished and with a fire blazing merrily in the grate. By necessity, we all stood in front of it, warming our freezing hands.

"How kind of you to come," said Mrs Canty. "My trinkets, I suppose, would fetch little at auction, but I attach great sentimental value to them. None could ever be replaced, you see. Gloria Lamb is heartbroken over the affair. Her diamond engagement ring and a pair of her mother's matching ruby earrings are missing, and yet, why should this thief choose to ignore my husband's wallet, his gold repeater and cufflinks? There was some valuable plate in the next room also."

Holmes smiled, lighting his pipe and tossing the match into the flames, his eyes bent low upon the glow of the fire.

"I think I can offer a plausible explanation, madam," said he. "Perhaps the burglar was only interested in gemstones?"

"Why, I had never thought of it quite like that, Mr Holmes," she confided, picking up her Scotch terrier and patting its head affectionately.

"A jackdaw of sorts?" I interjected.

"Yes, a very apt description, my dear Watson," said my colleague, tapping the stem of his pipe upon the mantelpiece. He then turned to Reginald Canty who sat by the fire, a golden-haired spaniel curled at his feet, listening to all that had been said with a keen interest.

"Could I borrow your ladder? It will only be for a half-hour or so."

"The ladder?" Mr Canty exclaimed.

"I wish to climb on to the roof. What about you, Watson? Are you game?"

"Certainly," said I, putting on my gloves:

"Then I shall ask Matthews to fetch it," said Canty,

ringing for the servant.

"Capital. I shall start with the Lambs' house next door and work my way round," my companion remarked, getting ready to leave.

Simplicity and utility were evidently in Svenson's mind when he designed the Lambs' house, for it could quite easily have passed for a customs post on the Swiss frontier. Less hybrid than Canty's dwelling, it possessed a high shelf, or platform, on the roof, apparently once designated to become a glass-domed observatory, but which, according to Canty, never materialised on account of its prohibitive cost and the widespread criticism the project received from the local population. Great icicles hung from the porch and the glow from the lantern made the snow shimmer like polished diamonds, for a hard frost had set in.

Philip Lamb answered the door in his dressing gown. He was a thin, wiry individual, with swept-back silver hair and spectacles. His beady eyes examined us over a large, hawkish nose.

"You are Mr Sherlock Holmes, I take it?"

"I am. And this is my companion, Dr Watson. Your wife took things rather badly, I hear."

"I am afraid that is the case. Are you coming in? My wife is in the music room at present, so you shan't disturb her. I presume you do want to see the bedroom?" he said, looking suspiciously at Matthews and the long ladder he was carrying.

"I don't think that will be necessary, Mr Lamb. However, I should like to get on to your roof, if I may?"

"My roof!" The bank manager seemed taken aback by this request.

"Perfectly so. As you can see, Mr Canty has kindly supplied a ladder from next door for that same purpose."

"Surely you are not implying that the thief some-how managed to scale the side of my house, Mr Holmes? Why, he should require the physiognomy of a multi-taloned insect, sir!"

"I doubt whether the thief was transmuted into a fly, Mr Lamb. Though I grant you he has a most ambidextrous mind. If I were you, I should shut the door, you'll catch the death of cold standing out here!" Lamb stuck his glasses firmly upon his nose, gave my friend a quizzical, uncertain stare and closed his ._ door. Without delay, we went round to the side of the house and the ladder was leaned against the wall and manoeuvred into position by Matthews.

"This is preposterous, Watson!" said Holmes, gazing up at the wall. "See how the blanket of snow on the ledge and timbers remains undisturbed?"

"We shall need some sort of light up there," said I.

"I have the very thing, sir, a dark lantern. I took the precaution of bringing it along with me," said the manservant.

"You excel yourself, Matthews!" said Holmes, snatching the lamp and clambering up the ladder.

I eventually managed to climb over some parapets and scramble onto the roof, and there I could vaguely discern the bent figure of Holmes, his hawk-like features lit up by the gleam of the lamp, poring over the snow with his magnifying lens.

"I do not possess a spirit level, Watson, but tell me what you make of the window to the loft, will you?"

"Why, both sliding sections do not run true with the sill," said I.

"Yes, and the window frame is only lightly pinned in and should lift away easily from the wall with the aid of a chisel. You will observe how the lime-based mortar has not been mixed properly and the bricks around the window needs repointing!"

"Thanks to the British speculative builder, the housebreaker has no need of a glass cutter these days!" said I, incredulously. "He simply removes the entire window - glass panels and all!"

"And replaces it afterwards. Yes, that's how he got in, Watson, and yet I cannot fathom how on earth he got up here in the first place."

Suddenly, his bewildered expression was trans-posed to one of glee. He rushed over to one of the par-apets and, scraping away the fresh layer of fallen snow with his hand, sifted what lay beneath through his fingers and placed something in his pocket.

"Ha, this fellow is certainly no ordinary lark, Watson!"

"I think it's about time this jackdaw had his wings clipped a little," said I.

"Yes, we must get down from this great height and search out his nest, for I am certain it is there we shall find the missing gems."

We left Matthews to retrieve the ladder and went straight away next door where Canty and his wife were both sat with their dogs, anxiously awaiting our return.

"Do you know of Colonel Bradstock-Hume?" said Holmes, warming his frozen hands by the fire.

Canty thought for a moment and lit his cigar. "Do you mean the engineer responsible for the Lyneham Bridge?"

"That is the very man," replied Holmes.

"Not personally, although I believe he is something of a local celebrity and lives over in Radstone at Compton Old Hall, Mr Holmes, just a few stops down the line from Haversham."

"I see. Well, I should like to pay this Colonel Bradstock-Hume a visit."

"I think you shall find him away at present - in Tunisia, working on a dam."

"Are there many trains to Radstone?"

"One train every hour up until midnight, but I can assure you, Mr Holmes, your visit to Radstone would be a wasted one, for according to the Surrey Gazette, the Colonel will be away for several weeks."

———

The train to Radstone was already standing in the platform when we arrived at the station. We hurriedly collected our tickets and went straight away to a waiting carriage.

"Good gracious, Holmes," said I, as we each lit a cigarette. "What has Colonel Bradstock-Hume got to do with all this? Has the thief somehow managed to conceal his hoard upon the Colonel's property? If so, I'm damned if I know how you discovered it."

"It is the Colonel himself that interests me, Watson. He is a keen sportsman and, it so happens, I recall reading about one of his exploits in The Telegraph last year."

"Has he fallen on hard times and needs the swag to see him through? I suppose he'll get a few hundred pounds for his night's haul - if he's lucky, that is."

"Oh, he is wealthy enough."

"Then what was his motive?"

"It is elementary, my dear Watson. The colonel believed he could commit the perfect crime and get away with it. However, our jackdaw's wings are about to be clipped and I have not the slightest intention of allowing him to get off lightly!"

We alighted at Radstone Station and immediately went and enquired of the porter the exact whereabouts of Compton Old Hall and were accordingly directed down a steep hill. It was a frosty night and the road remained an unbroken white line - a gleaming icy surface, pavements frozen and hedgerow trees over-arched with snow. At the bottom of the hill, I observed a large country house, partly disguised by trees, its gabled roof glittering under the softening light of the moon. This was evidently Compton Old Hall, the residence of Colonel Bradstock-Hume.

We arrived at the lodge gates and were trudging up the drive when a light glimmered and a burly individual emerged from the shadows of the entrance porch holding a lamp. I heard a barn owl screeching from the tall oaks bordering the park, followed by a low whistle, and instinctively reached for my service revolver, for out of the blackness, two large and ferocious Dobermanns came bounding towards us.

"Come away, Rex!" a voice then shouted coarsely. "And you, Salter! Come back, I say, at once."

The dogs obediently turned on their heels and went trotting back to their master, no doubt happy for the exercise.

"You, there, sir!" the figure shouted, pointing in my direction. "You are trespassing on my property! Kindly leave the grounds and take your friend there with you."

"I presume that it is Colonel Bradstock-Hume of Compton Old Hall I have the pleasure of addressing?" said Holmes, with a most reposeful air.

The colonel, whose massive stature was daunting, trudged over to greet us. The dogs circled about his great ham-thighs, their eyes glinting menacingly.

"Ah, now I see you are both gentlemen." He held out his hand. "I apologise for my rough manner. At first, I took you to be a couple of jemmy-bashers come to set about my fine plate and blow my safe. Though, I confess, I have never met either of you before. Have you come about the Istanbul contract?"

"I have come about a burglary in Haversham, Colonel," said Holmes, sternly.

The engineer's jaw dropped and he instantly averted his gaze from my companion's, preferring to look at the ground instead.

"You are the police, I take it?" he muttered. Holmes, with a thin smile upon his lips, deliberately allowed Bradstock-Hume to ruminate of his guilty secret for a while, and after about fifteen seconds had elapsed said quietly: "No, we are not."

The relief on the engineer's face was evident. "I think you'd both better come inside and share a blast of fire."

We passed up a snow-covered flight of steps and were led into a warm, spacious oak-panelled room filled with the dense reek of cigar smoke. There was a desk covered with the detailed plans of various engineering projects the Colonel had undertaken and we waded across rolls of drawing paper, large reference works, set squares and the like, to a pair of handsome Jacobean chairs, set either side of the fireplace.

"Do take a seat," said he.

He poured us a glass of whisky and soda each and, lounging in front of the hearth with his dogs, said matter-of-factly: "You will observe, gentlemen, that I possess a number of glass-sided cabinets containing all manner of intricate brass models, supplied with working parts and built by myself, mostly for exhibitions. There is an American Wild West locomotive and a fireman's pump engine. Place a penny in the slot and the wheels shall start spinning, else a piston rod gyrate back and forth."

Rex and Salter lay stretched on a large Turkey rug, watching their master with gleaming, baleful eyes by the light of the flickering coal fire.

"Ingenious!" Holmes replied. "But, I have no pennies and besides, more pressing matters must be seen to!"

"What are your names?" asked the Colonel.

"Sherlock Holmes," replied my friend, "and this is my colleague, Dr Watson."

"Indeed, I should be interested to learn why on earth you chose to waste your time - and mine - by coming out here on a freezing night to discuss these burglaries in Haversham, Mr Holmes."

"Burglaries - did I mention more than one? I don't believe I did!" said my colleague with a whimsical smile.

"Oh, I read something about it in the East Surrey Chronicle," he answered in a slovenly way.

"Wasn't it the *Surrey Gazette*?"

"Of course."

"Well, that's a queer thing, because the matter was deliberately kept discreet and no article appeared in any of the papers. I shall speak plainly, Colonel Bradstock-Hume. I have come here to Compton Old Hall tonight because I know you to be the thief. Come now, man, admit it! You have already committed a prize blunder."

"Nonsense!" replied the colonel, irately, but before he could say another word, Holmes put up his hand and waved all objections aside.

"And I have more than a grain of evidence to prove it." Holmes came and stood behind the colonel's chair, placed his hand into his pocket and retrieved a damp ball of fine-grained sand of a deep reddish colour, which he carefully sifted through his long, bony fingers and spread over the armrest. "Excellent ballast, wouldn't you agree, Colonel?"

The proud soldier slumped back in his chair and grew very pale.

"One of your sacks was most likely damaged when you made your descent and landed upon the observatory platform. Watson, come over here, will you? I have something to show you."

I joined my colleague by the window and as I glanced out of the black pane, there, in the park behind the colonel's house, I was amazed to see an air balloon, with taut ropes and grapnel hooks holding it to the ground, and sacks of ballast dangling from the basket suspended beneath.

"Masterly! If Charlie Peace were alive, I am sure he would play his fiddle for you, Colonel!"

"I am glad you seem so amused, Mr Holmes. I am wondering whether my little aeronautical adventure has ended on a sour note, though I'm damned if I haven't met an equal in you! Tell me, sir, am I for the county jail, or what is it worth to you and your fine friend here to keep me out? I am wealthy enough to offer you a good envelope each for your trouble."

"That will not be necessary, Colonel. You are acquainted with the Scandinavian architect Frederik Svenson, I take it?"

"Ah, I see where this is leading, Mr Holmes. Yes, he seeks my advice from time to time about structural problems arising from his often complex and radical designs."

"And, I recall, you collaborated together on the much criticised Stenback Opera House in Helsinki?"

"Fredi owns a ferro-concrete bungalow, designed by himself, at the western end of Lake Utsjoki. I stayed with him when I was working on the plans for the opera house and it was there, whilst enjoying a Finnish bath, that he slung a tub of water over the hot stones and asked me the following question: 'Do you know of the Haversham development?' I told him I lived nearby and had read about it in the Society's journal and he, thereafter, boasted that all three of the houses he had designed were burglar proof, for he employed a unique system of shutters and all the locks and catches were manufactured to his own specification. I warned him not to underestimate the ingenuity of the English criminal class, for invariably their motto was 'Where there's a will, there's a way' and, to a perpetual egoist like himself, this was tantamount to being challenged to a duel. He immediately laid down odds, and hefty ones they were too, I might add, that no thief could possibly accomplish such a thing. Being fond of a bet, I decided to have a go myself.

"To overcome the problem of locks and latches, upon my return to this country I paid a visit to the Guildford firm of White and Perry, who originally carried out the work, and managed to obtain some useful information. Over a pipe, Perry - a near-neighbour of mine - showed me the plans and pointed out that in order to cut corners, and thereby make an enormous profit, amongst other areas of skimped workmanship, certain of the attic windows were not provided with outer shutters, nor were the frames, to his knowledge, set properly into the wall. They were high up and awkwardly placed, but the unique pitch of the roofs and, in one case, the redundant observatory platform, would make the task of burglaring the houses much easier than I had at first envisaged.

"Svenson did not wish to part with his money easily and one of his impossible provisos stated that the burglary must take place when the houses were occupied. Another was that all three should be burgled together!

"The more I thought about it, the less hopeful I became, and then I struck upon the bright idea of incorporating my hot-air balloon into the scheme of things. Flying has always been a passion of mine and I thought perhaps, with room to manoeuvre, I might conceivably vault over the trees, land on the observatory platform and then hop over to the others. The last week in December, I telegraphed Svenson and arranged to meet him here at my house on New Year's Eve. He accompanied me on my criminal escapade as overseer, to make sure fair play was in order, and, as a consequence, departed for Ostend this morning with his tail between his legs - several thousand pounds the poorer - having lost his bet, but with a good deal more respect for the Englishman than ever he owned before our little adventure!"

"I presume you were about to make another trip tonight and return the missing jewellery?"

"It was to have been my hundredth ascent. However, not wishing to tempt fate a second time, I should have landed on Deacons Common at midnight and legged it across the woods from there. I have in my possession three separate packets, each containing the missing gems. I had intended to place them on the doorsteps, to be reclaimed by the ladies tomorrow morning!"

"Whilst I appreciate your verve and tenacity in seeking to aspire to the perfect crime, you failed to appreciate the feelings of others."

"You'll inform the police, then, Mr Holmes?" said he, realising for the first time the full gravity of the situation.

"No, although you shall have some honest explaining to do when we return to Haversham, for these ladies are to be your judge and jury, Colonel Bradstock-Hume."

The old gentleman frowned. "Very well then, if it is to be a 'petticoat court' I must face, so be it. I should prefer to take my chances there than with a real one."

"The recovery of the stolen jewellery and an extremely generous donation to the ladies' favourite poor charity might help swing the balance in your favour. I shall, of course, accompany you to the hearing with Dr Watson here, who is himself a very lenient judge of character!"

The colonel seemed much relieved. "I suppose we had better catch the train - there is one in ten minutes upon the hill."

"Oh, a train!" said Holmes, somewhat caustically. "You disappoint me!"

"Ah, you wish to survey the old market town of Haversham from a great height?" answered the colonel, laughing heartily. "There is nothing quite like a flight in an air balloon. The sensation is most agreeable and complimentary to the digestive organs, Dr Watson!"

And so we flew in an air balloon, and drifted upon the air currents for a quarter hour until we began our descent and landed on Deacons Common. I was disappointed that our journey had come to an end so soon, for the view of the Surrey hills from that great height, with the lights of the houses glittering like diamonds beneath, was truly magnificent to behold.

The Dutch Steamship Friesland

THE SCRAPING, long drawn-out dirge, a discordant off-key rendition so termed 'experimental' had been occupying my friend upon his violin for the last hour at least, a look of unalloyed bliss softening his features whilst he assiduously studied the score propped on his deal chemistry table.

I flung my newspaper at the fireguard and exclaimed, "Enough of Blake's tortuous descent into the abyss, Holmes. Cannot you instead play a snatch of Mendelssohn or Weber?"

"A master work by the Czech composer Janik Krezler evoking serenity," said he.

Making a grab for the scorched pages of The Times scattered on the hearth rug I resumed my chair.

"Could you not detect the subtlety, Watson?"

"He is welcome to that damn row," I retorted, aggrieved by the inference I was dull to music.

However, upon this occasion we did not remain at loggerheads and my fellow lodger complied with my request which was not ordinarily the case. A most uplifting and professionally played violin air swept about our room, bringing me close to tears, and so continued for ten or so minutes.

Such had been our morning, snow falling outside the bay, settling in heaps upon the lintel, more of a driving torrent of snow, actually, not the best weather to be out in, although shortly we should be compelled to leave the warmth of our rooms, braving the inclement conditions thus to visit Bradleys the tobacconist along Oxford Street, for I found myself running low of my favourite 'Ships', Holmes his oily black shag and our supply of cigarettes was virtually depleted.

Quite abruptly, Mr Sherlock Holmes abandoned his playing, scowling out of the sitting room window, Stradivarius still tucked under his sharp chin, bow held across fretboard.

"Not much to see on a day such as this, old chap," said I, "and we shall soon be out in it."

"On the contrary, dear fellow, I perceive below a carriage has halted outside the front door to our diggings. I cannot, alas, make out a clear figure, though somebody proceeds through the snow to the front step. Ah, the doorbell rings - we have a visitor."

Footfalls upon the stair, normally of no cause for concern, prompted a nervy alertness. I was certainly on my guard, for Holmes had recently, in the last week, put a violent gang leader, Josh Toker, behind bars for life. I personally loathed these after-trial periods of uncertainty, part of the business of catching criminals, for his consultancy was not without its detractors; he had enemies, after all. Now, at his insistence, I kept my service revolver handy and he a small pistol in the pocket of his dressing gown. Upon this occasion, however, I am glad to report we had nothing to fear. A grinning, boyish face, both honest and open, peeped round the door, a strapping blond, nut-brown chap wearing a full-length, beaver-skin coat holding an Astrakhan fur hat strode across and shook hands.

"I perceive by your chronographic gold wristwatch, exclusive to Bergums of Oslo, a company specialising in shipboard nautical instruments of the finest balance. Are you Norwegian, perchance?"

"My name is Kristian Haraldsen," said he, removing his heavy fur coat and gloves. "I am indeed from Norway. You are Mr Sherlock Holmes. I read about your solving the Princess Eva case, her jewels stolen from the Albert Hall where she attended a concert in her honour and I was much impressed. I am to deliver a lecture at your Royal Geographical Society this evening. Mr Markham, the Vice President, kindly proposed a grant of three hundred pounds towards my expedition."

"Watson and I are honorary members of the R.G.S. You are involved in polar exploration; such a time-piece, the chrono-graphic watch you wear indicates this to me."

"I am to lead a scientific mission, an expedition to the Arctic. My vessel, a non-chartered ex-Dutch owned steamship, the Friesland, has been undergoing an extensive refit, conversion to an ice-breaker, the hull reinforced, more powerful engines, larger coal bunkers. It has cost much, but is totally necessary and her fitting out is now completed. That said, a number of peculiarities, which I wish to discuss, have arisen. I am currently in London and felt a visit to your flat at 221 B Baker Street, a short stroll from my hotel, might provide me with some answers."

"Your explorer compatriot, Fridjof Nansen, is of course known to me, although, as you will be aware, he devotes his life more to politics now."

Allowing an interval for our landlady to share round cups and pour coffee, to offer a plate of biscuits, all well appreciated. Mrs Hudson scuttled out, closing the door quietly behind her. Meanwhile, I took the opportunity to heap more coals onto the fire, stabbing it repeatedly with the poker to liven up the flames, interested to hear how the conversation would progress.

My colleague chose his long Cherry-wood pipe from the rack and, settling back in his armchair, proceeded to smoke.

"You refer to peculiarities; these are of a criminal intent, I presume?" he enquired. "Stay with the facts if you will, Mr Haraldsen, then we might better reach the core of your problem."

Placing his coffee cup upon the arm of the chair, the Norwegian replied succinctly, "Having, with my associates and the Norwegian government, purchased the Dutch steam vessel, a 678 ton whaler, I went about the monumental task of overseeing her refit for Arctic exploration. Now, Mr Holmes," he sighed, "my office has been broken into. I have grown suspicious that persons without my knowledge have boarded the ship berthed in Oslo. Our loading, stacking of the tonnage of supplies necessary for the voyage north is done during the day. The vessel is not, at present, used as living quarters and yet late at night lights have been observed, movement on and below deck, but when I check on. board, all is well, correct and shipshape, no trace of stowaways. My crew, a group of talented scientists and seagoing specialists, only laugh at my concern, blaming overwork. These men, I know, are to be trusted and relied on."

"You are wise to be cautious; I recall a quite substantial coaler, the S.S. Dorsland, stolen in Brazil, never consequently traced, just one instance of reported maritime crime. Pirates in modern form still flourish. Your ex-whaler, turned expedition vessel, is, I trust, insured?"

"The expedition's finance is not an issue, sir. I am wealthy, for I inherited my family's canning interests. The vessel's refit was part funded by my government, but what I require, Mr Holmes, is your expertise, your assistance to establish if a crime is being evolved. My office has been broken into three times now, but would you, on such a whim as mine, even be prepared to come to Norway to take on the case?"

My colleague knocked his pipe out in the ashtray. "Your request is timely, Mr Haraldsen, for I shall be frank and admit I am myself rather pressed at present due to my being responsible for the recent incarceration of a gang leader, Josh Toker, whose criminal associates wish me disposed of in a drum of acid. Mr Toker being detained at Her Majesty's pleasure indefinitely on my evidence means it might be prudent to take a brief sojourn abroad, to be absent from London awhile. For a fee, I should be prepared to aid your cause."

"You have my word all your expenses shall be met, Mr Holmes."

"So, let us consider the probability that persons have indeed boarded your ship, loitering on the vessel. I should thereby conjecture a number of your so-called trusted, hand-picked expedition members are *not* to be trusted. Your normal practice is to place advertisements in the newspapers when recruiting, I take it?"

"I did, but I will emphasise not all of the crew were selected and interviewed from answering advertisements. Certain of my men, who show a strong unity of purpose, I have known previously."

"Granted, but that process of recruitment in itself leaves you vulnerable. What I imply is that you unwittingly may have allowed a nest of vipers to infiltrate your assembly. Outwardly, these people who applied no doubt would seem exemplary candidates for your scientific mission, brimful of enthusiasm for your project, yet in reality perhaps certain from the selection of your party are bent upon a shocking subterfuge, for that expensively kitted expedition vessel represents a ready-made convenient means of smashing through pack ice to unload tons of equipment on the sea ice to establish a base, a depot somewhere. The nature of the crime we cannot yet determine."

"When I administer expeditions, Mr Holmes, I take into account the psychology of personnel, considering what problems of leadership I may encounter," explained Haraldsen. "Each successful candidate must be physically fit and possess that equable nature so necessary to the vicissitudes of polar travel, but there could be hidden agendas, certainly."

"Presumably these individuals, were they intent on taking over your ship, should be aware of both the topographical and scientific proclivities of the area of the Arctic they intend to visit. Experts in their field they would have to be."

"But Holmes, nothing save whales of any import exists in those far-off freezing wastes," said I, lighting my pipe to smoke the last of my tobacco. "Begging your pardon, Kristian, but I am at a total loss why anybody, let alone criminals, should care to venture so far north."

"I suggest, after your Royal Geographical Society lecture, Watson and myself shall, along with our baggage, accompany you, Mr Haraldsen, to catch the express boat train, thence the ferry to the port of Oslo in Norway. While you are concerned with your talk, I shall seek out one whose ability to regain facts regarding maps and geography equals that of my brother, Mycroft, concerning political analysis and matters pertaining to the state where questions concerning anomalies of land mass and the world's oceans are concerned."

That evening, having been occupied with packing our carpet bags, making preparations for the journey to Scandinavia, we hastened across London, the hansom with the carriage lamps aglow, bell jangling, contributing to more and more wheel ruts caused by other horse-drawn traffic churning the crisp layer of white snow then encompassing the capital's streets.

Lit by rows of shop fronts, the snowy pavement revealed those well wrapped up venturing abroad, bound for a night out at the Variety Theatre, else seeking the conviviality of public houses.

Ascending the steps to the portico-fronted entrance of the Royal Geographical Society at No. 1 Savile Row, the announced lecture concerning the Northwest Passage in front of a seven-hundred-strong audience did not concern us, rather drawn to the oak-panelled members' library along the way containing an unrivalled collection of atlases, maps and travel literature, the groaning, sagging shelves burdened with prestigious amounts of calf-bound rarities and first editions. Rooms where hung portraits in oils of past presidents of the R.G.S., notable global explorers, and as should be expected in such a prestigious institution, a picture of Her Majesty the Queen above the mantelshelf. Grave, superior faces quivering by firelight strangely alive, imposing their lofty presence, adding to the profound sense of history of the place.

On our approach, Cedric Bitten, the long-serving secretary and senior librarian of this members' sanctuary, got up from his desk, tottering over, stooped by his great age, wearing the thickest-lensed spectacles I ever saw to aid combat his failing sight. He peered myopically. "Why, Mr Holmes," said he,

"what an unexpected pleasure to see you; you also, Watson. The Norwegian's lecture proves too long-winded, tiring to follow? I sympathise. Nansen was difficult to hear, Amundsen's English atrocious. Shall I ring for coffee?

"Please do. My dear Bitten, might I wrack your knowledgeable brains concerning the Arctic?"

"Of course, so many of our members are headed that way, else have explored the Arctic in the past. I have made a specialist study of both Poles. What is it you require to know?"

Holmes pursed his thin lips, passing round his silver cigarette case. Bitten accepted a Bradley's, lit the tip with his brass petrol lighter, his skull-like, cadaverous features accentuated by the wavering flame. "Do you, perchance, recall encountering anything remotely of consequence to a criminal fraternity? I confess, I and Watson are at somewhat of a loss. Seals, polar bears need hardly be considered."

"None that I can recall from books or maps, but please pass over to the wallchart, gentlemen. Allow me to mull over any notable possibilities ... gold, for instance," said he at length, giving us a quizzical look. "By Jove, yes," cried Holmes excitedly, watching the aged librarian's gnarled finger stab upon an area of inked-in curly waves.

"Do not, I beg you, Mr Holmes, hold out the slight-est hope of it being recoverable, else of any use to a criminal organisation. A rumour, hearsay, once told me over a glass of sherry at the society's club by old Leigh Smith, a fascinating chap who explored the westerly part of Franz Josef Land in his English yacht Eira, making many discoveries concerning valuable marine and botanical life of note. His yacht sank, forc-ing Smith to winter on one of the islands; had a crew mate, an Eskimo, who related that it was traditionally believed by his race that the seabed of the Bering Sea was rife with a boundless resource of pure gold resting just beneath the surface of the shale bed, and yet no one should, alas, ever profit, for it was impossible to reach those depths conserving the thick layers of plate ice, the temperature of sea water in those regions. So no gold, not for the enterprising crooks, nor anyone else, I'm afraid."

"Mining the gold should be out of the question, Bitten?"

"Absolutely, Mr Holmes. No nation on earth, however large their industrial might, could provide the means, no human being survive being submerged in frozen brash ice or plumbing the depths of the Bering Sea. But let us not forget, either, that this rumour of gold may be but a myth - hence my caution."

The R.G.S. doorman, Albert Jardine, bundling us into a four-wheeler cab along with our baggage, wished us all the best, and whilst sat in the carriage after broaching the topic of gold in the Bering Sea to Mr Haraldsen, my colleague was met with quiet incredulity, thereafter revealing his lively, effervescent personality the Norwegian at first understood Holmes' claim to be more of a joke.

"I can countenance mineral deposits yet to be discovered north of the Arctic Circle, but gold at the bottom of the Bering Sea defies belief. This Eskimo you talk of was no doubt repeating some old wives' tale to make children's eyes light up round the camp fire, a legend more beholden to the Ice Queen, I suspect," said Mr Haraldsen as we rattled along in our cab to the station to catch the night express. "Scandinavian folklore is full of such tales."

"Although, if a way existed to get at that dratted gold, surely criminals should be first to find it, and that ship of yours, the *Friesland*, should be of great assistance attaining the region."

"Holmes, why look so serious? Come on, this theory of yours is plainly unsustainable."

"From past experience, my dear Kristian, I should not be so inclined to dismiss such an enterprise as wholly impossible. If only Forster, that Kansas mining engineer, was still at the Langham. I know him socially, as does Watson. He is a fine, bright fellow, but I believe gone back to the United States. We could have in practical terms discussed the possibility of deep water mining."

"That is so," I answered, stuffing some 'Ships' into my briar pipe as we rattled along, "yet Forster is a first-rate talent at oil wells. Mining beneath the frozen tundra should be another matter."

"Let it go, Mr Holmes," implored the Norwegian good-humouredly. "There's surely better theories to come once we arrive at Oslo and you can interview the crew and see my expedition ship, the Friesland, for yourselves."

We spent what remained of the afternoon on the first day of our arrival in Oslo being shown onto the deck of Mr Haraldsen's expedition vessel, the ex-Dutch steamship, Friesland, berthed in the harbour within sight of the Royal Palace along the waterfront. A programme of loading stores by wharf-side crane then in progress, barrels of paraffin, crates of boat gear, clothing, pallets stacked with every canned and packaged rations imaginable swung on board.

While Sherlock Holmes was lost to the bowels of the ship, concerning himself making a survey of the below-decks quarters and storage, for myself, I was perfectly content to walk about with Kristian, impressed at the picked crew and scientific team's camaraderie, the obvious respect shown to their leader, Herr Haraldsen.

Later, my esteemed colleague, rake thin, in fact taller than any of the expedition party, joined us in the wheelhouse for a mug of coffee. He had been gone three-quarters of an hour and appeared wan and thoughtful.

"So, Mr Holmes, now you intend to tell me it's all been a complete waste of time, and I've unfairly summoned you over here to Oslo on an absurd whim with little foundation," laughed the polar explorer, pouring steaming coffee for us all before passing round his tobacco pouch. "I'm an ass, in other words." "On the contrary, Mr Haraldsen," warned Holmes, taking out his pipe. "You must remain vigilant, not a word to your compatriots, nor even Captain Vigeland, mind. Not a whiff of police activity. As agreed previously, Watson and myself are simply a batty pair of invited Englishmen from the Royal Geographical Society allowed to see how the expedition is progressing. Now, when I first came aboard yesterday, I was alerted by an old tried trick, for I found a large-sized tin of Colman's mustard powder in a grocer's box kept in your pantry store, weightier than the rest. The tin rattled, thus, methodical in my approach, prising open the lid I discovered a number of American quick-locking handcuffs, presumably of slim value when hunting seals on the ice floes, but most advantageous when holding a group of men hostage aboard ship.

You are in dire peril. You sail when?"

"At the end of next week."

"Then we must penetrate this business long before then."

———

Preceding dinner in the hotel restaurant, haddock followed by apple cake and a fine Gamalost cheese, I and my esteemed colleague retired upstairs to our rooms to smoke our pipes and sample the local aquavit. However, to such as he, relaxing was an anathema -work most assuredly came before leisure.

"Watson, we must endeavour to discover more about the applicants. Tomorrow I shall identify those members of Haraldsen's team who answered from an advertisement. For now, though, I am inclined to walk off that hearty dinner we enjoyed in the restaurant. I think we shall stroll along the waterfront; the harbour is nearby our hotel anyhow. Haraldsen is, I believe, on board the Friesland supervising the loading of sledges with broad runners. We are to liaise tomorrow at breakfast."

"Holmes," I pointed out, "you have neglected your pipe for the last half hour."

"I assure you I shall not neglect my pipe on my return, however. I have much to ponder regarding the possibility of a ship being stolen under the very nose of Kristian Haraldsen."

"Well," said I, "there are surely very few of these icebreakers in existence. The rarity of such a specialised craft capable of penetrating north to the arctic is of immense value to a foe."

"Exemplary. Having back at our diggings in Baker Street consulted a Lloyds shipping broker's yearly report I kept on file, very out of date but useful for my needs, I was interested to learn of two separate incidences of piracy, each involving a vessel being hijacked out at sea, the genuine crew overcome by force thence thrown overboard. This, I surmise, represents the preferable method the criminals are intending to adopt."

"And old Bitten' s gold theory still stands."

"It does."

Oslo harbour, being situated at the end of an inner fjord crowded with small islands, surrounded by extensive forests, as should be expected at this season, the cold air outside was bracing, the city's setting charmingly clad in snow. Holmes and myself, at Mr Haraldsen' s insistence, had been kitted out with hefty seamen's coats and fur boots, the flaps of Holmes' familiar deerstalker I can vouch tied beneath his chin to protect his ears from the severe chill.

We were, I recall, strolling alongside a row of sheds when I beheld, in front a hatted individual striding purposefully, smoking a cigar, a somewhat reluctant chimpanzee secured on a dog lead, loping through the snow beside him; a somewhat bizarre sight. My friend, making certain we kept the fellow in view, knelt down upon the walkway briefly to retrieve dropped cigar ash. Crumbling the tobacco between gloved fingers, Holmes proclaimed expertly, "Square Villigers, Swiss - why, Morcroft Forster smokes that brand of pocket cigars. The wide-brimmed Stetson seems dratted familiar also."

"From the back it most certainly could be Forster, while in London a habitue at the Langham. I wonder where the American is headed. It's perfectly conceivable the Kansas geologist is working over here in Norway on a freelance basis. His job is, after all, mineral exploration, but for heaven's sake, Holmes, why the chimp?"

"Spare your condemnation, Watson. It will be understood Morcroft Forster is given hopelessly to being eccentric; one assumes, therefore, this is a tame pet, although the Langham has very strict rules regarding apes on the premises, so he must have purchased the animal at a pet store in Oslo."

The fellow in front of us, along with his chimp, ducked into a side entrance belonging to a warehouse, one of numerous along the waterfront.

Hurrying ahead, Holmes, using his propelling pencil, scribbled against the wall a short note requesting Forster should visit our Oslo hotel, the Akershus, at the earliest oppor-tunity, additionally supplying the room number. He placed it in a convenient icicle laden mailbox capped with snow.

The warehouse door was partly open and we were able to glimpse a vast, brightly-lit workshop space busy with activity, a stack of crates marked Westinghouse Corporation. This before our path was blocked by an immense Afro-Caribbean man, broad of shoulder with a hugely developed muscular chest and ham fists. I myself felt threatened, but my colleague, Sherlock Holmes, stared incredulously into the handsome, resolute face. "Why, Joe Dixie!" said he cheerfully. "You went ten rounds with Hull's Alf 'Slugger' Dodds at Brighton racecourse. I was in the crowd cheering you on. Joe, you're one of the finest bare-knuckle boxers ever to grace the ring. What brings you to Oslo?"

I was aware Hof a clicking, whirring of mechanism. "Hi boss, hi boss, hi boss," the voice intoned in a tinny way, "how ya doin', doin', doin', how ya."

The warehouse door slammed in our faces leaving us none the wiser regarding what had become of the Kansas geologist, but the name 'Westinghouse' offered a useful explanation.

"I have it," said I, cleaning out the stem of my 'bent apple' briar pipe by means of a goose feather and spirit of meths, sat comfortably before the rumbling woodstove in our hotel room, much invigorated after our walk round the docks.

"Really," murmured Holmes indifferently, puffing on his pipe, gazing grimly out of the window at the lights of Oslo twinkling into the far distance, a glass of Aquavit close to hand, mostly lost in his own thoughts, for I detected something was bothering him.

"Listen, Westinghouse Corporation is responsible for lighting up America from coast to coast; power generators of immense voltage, light bulbs and God knows what."

"Allowing for Westinghouse vacuum air brakes fitted to locomotives, but go on Watson, I likewise observed, or rather glimpsed, all those various-sized packing crates back at the warehouse. Those are what you're referring to, I take it."

"George Westinghouse is called the Electricity King. His business empire extends round the globe. What could be simpler, more obvious? Our American chum, Forster, whom we saw the back of, is working over here for a spell, his expertise useful in the laying of power lines."

"And the chimp?"

"A blasted pet of no consequence," I retorted. "You said so yourself, Holmes."

"Alas, I have reason to change my opinion," said my friend seriously, knocking out the smoky ash from his pipe on the lip of a china hotel vase. "I'd rather it were not the case, of course, but the monkey, I am sure, will be experimented on. I dread to think how many other such apes are given their daily walks, keeping up their health, before being returned to numbered cages."

"A preposterous supposition."

"I think not; allow me then to firstly refresh your memory the one-time celebrity, the Austrian, Paul Kemphlar."

Leaning back in his armchair, my rake-thin colleague proceeded to steeple his long, sensitive fingers together, gazing at me with bright, perceptive eyes set each side of a great raptor' s beak of a nose while the stove rumbled on.

"You will recall the newspaper article four years ago recording the visit of the Prince of Wales to the great Exhibition at Crystal Palace."

"I do not," said I bluntly.

"We visited ourselves, and indeed had the oppor-tunity of solving a number of crimes in the vicinity of Upper Norwood. But I digress. Paul Kemphlar, the brilliant creator of clockwork and electrical automata, so received were his works that the Prince of Wales paid a special visit to his stand, heaping praise upon the young inventor, the Paris Exhibition alike a suc-cess, crowds overwhelming."

"Dolls?" I queried, reaching for my glass of schnapps.

"A 'life-size', a personification of a foot soldier in the ranks of Napoleon's army, cocked tricorn hat, uniform exact, so conceived it could salute, blink, and raise its rifle. Hundreds of thousands of visitors to the Crystal Palace were amazed, unable to accept the soldier was not a clever actor, in reality mechanical, a fully-automated waxwork; Kemphlar, to hysterical applause, unscrewed the back, revealing the working parts, quelling the illusion. Feted by European royalty, so popular was his Napoleonic soldier he began, by public demand, to exhibit working replicas in prestigious department stores in Paris, London and New York. However, disaster struck at a toy store in Stockholm. One of the duplicates of the lifelike mechanical soldier malfunctioned, running amok amongst the shoppers, attempting to strangle a child, a little boy, lifting him clear off his feet in an attempt to throttle his neck. An alert assistant tore open the back panel, wrenching wires apart hence saving the day, terminating the battery source, fusing the valve arrangement, thus neutralising the automaton."

My colleague paused to light his long pipe, his face disappearing behind wreaths of tobacco smoke.

"Now, I shall briefly allude to the Westinghouse Corporation. Earlier, on board the Friesland, I most assiduously searched below decks for any evidence of criminal activity. I can report, Watson, the identical Westinghouse marked packing crates to those at the warehouse, attempts made to deface, to remove the stencilled letters, these crates in a stores aboard that ship under tarpaulin. We can thus surmise that, although in no way illegally funding this project, Westinghouse are intending to take advantage, testing many advanced engineering components at extremes of low temperature and exorbitant pressure. You follow?"

"I'm afraid at present you have the advantage of me, Holmes. I am not that clear as yet."

"My dear boy, certainly a lot to digest at one sitting. I shall enlighten you better in the morning after we have attacked a hearty breakfast and are well rested. Let us to bed, for we have an early start and a lengthy day before us."

I had not long got up from my armchair, Holmes having risen to proceed to the table where he had assembled a sheaf of notes, when a tremendous crash assailed our senses, shocking my nerves to a war pitch. The hotel door burst in, our rooms attacked by not one, I say, but a pair of black fellows, powerfully built and aggressive, in looks identical twins to Joe Dixie, showing the all-round athletic form of the professional pugilist. Brandishing ham fists like clubs, they lumbered forward, striking out clumsily, revealing massive biceps, veins like cords bulging out of their thick necks. Amid the splintered wood and glass, the room all but destroyed in their wake, their war cry a surprisingly tinny voiced 'hi boss -hi boss - hi boss - how ya -how ya-how ya-doin' -doin -doin'.'

My colleague, quick on his feet, was first to react, surpassing me with his martial arts reflexes, his training in the amateur ring as a welterweight boxer able to ram his swordstick straight and true - but with poor result, for the chap felt nothing, a glazed surface smooth and solid as a breastplate visible through the gaping rent to his ruined waistcoat, no blood issuing from the torn shirt and, despite the force of the lunge, not a scratch, my colleague's blade, however, bent out of true, ruining its worth as a weapon.

Having grasped my service revolver, determined not to waste shots, recalling Holmes' long diatribe about the Napoleonic soldier while my antagonist swiped his fist at me, I stepped aside, able to aim squarely at his lower back, blasting him just above the spine. There was the noise of crunching metal and I was glad, at least, to hear that confounded, irritating 'hi boss -hi boss - hi boss - how ya doing- doin' — doin' wind down to an incomprehensible drawl. A persistent electric buzzer sounded, thus flinging open a window those rascal boxing types clambered outside making haste across the hotel roof and were gone, leaving me astounded, doubting if I were not then existing in a futuristic nightmare.

———

"I shall, of course, pay all charges incumbent at reception on account of the door broken off its hinges, damaged furniture and fittings and loose wall plaster pertaining to your wrecked hotel room. The manager of the Akershus assures me you will be moved to another floor, Mr Holmes. Are you gentlemen ready to board the Friesland and toast our success in the wheelhouse with a glass of schnapps?"

Mr Haraldsen, Holmes' client, was clearly gratified by all he had heard at a briefing earlier over breakfast, which tallied with his own findings. "Six of my team, including a scientist, failed to show for an important meeting this morning, damning proof of their collusion in this disgraceful plan to pirate my icebreaker, the Friesland, out at sea, dispose of me and the rest before sailing north of the Arctic Circle in search of gold, a perilous exploit involving enormous risk that I should personally not wish to emulate."

"Watson and myself, alert to further mischief, at first light left our hotel and checked along by the wharf and I can vouch, Mr Haraldsen, the place where Forster and the chimp were seen was abandoned, the warehouse empty. Obviously representatives of Westinghouse Corporation, after last night's ill-conceived skirmish, decided to pull the plug, as it were, fearing police involvement. They, including the automata maker Paul Kemphlar, with all the equipment and primate cages, escaped by boarding their chartered ship moored close to the warehouse. I am certain this is the only way such a large amount of equipment and stores could vanish overnight. This represented their swiftest and best means of leaving Oslo, heading out to sea. We can thus conclude your expedition to the Arctic, once you have assembled further crew, can now move forward free of molestation. I'd wager Paul Kemphlar shall not be furthering his use of replicant marvels for gold prospecting."

"So these automata, sculptured with pliable, super-hardened body shells were being assembled as divers, machine-men capable of withstanding extreme low temperature and immersion at depth beneath the Bering Sea. Remarkable."

"Monkeys used to test actual human endurance beneath the ice," said I grimly, reflecting on the chim-panzee we saw destined for a freezing cold water tank.

"My dear Kristian, as Watson will attest, I have been a long-time supporter of Joe Dixie, the bare-knuckle prize fighter, having on occasion watched him train at his base in Fulham. Joe is a New Yorker, of course. My, that fellow is not only likely to be world champion but extremely savvy, for he must have made a fair penny out of Paul Kemphlar's request to be plaster-casted from head to foot."

"They wanted a streamlined, athletic build for these things."

"One presumes a hole is cut in the ice and these automata, controlled from above by George

Westinghouse's advanced engineering by means of underwater cable, they are able, with the addition of suction devices, to scour the shale bed for deposits of gold. I take my hat off for their daring scheme, but pirating a ship is just not on."

—————

After our glass of schnapps, we decided to investigate further down in the ship's hold. Apart from discovering a cache of arms in one of the specified Westinghouse crates, two more Joe Dixies turned up, hollow, the pliable body shells yet to have a metal skeleton and clockwork and electrical mechanisms placed inside.

I confess the temptation proved too irresistible.

Holmes kept one effigy for himself, to be shipped back to London and retained as a 'curio' at our chambers in Baker Street, to replace the old wax dummy by Oscar Meuniers used so effectively in the 'empty house' case involving the air gun. I can report Mr Haraldsen purloined the other to take back for his children at his home in Oslo.

The Gordon Square Case

THE FIRST WEEK IN DECEMBER, Mrs Lodesley, who lived over by Regents Park, came dashing into our rooms in some state of agitation. A harsh and persistent frost had settled overnight and when I awoke my bedroom was chilly with a layer of ice crystals formed upon the window. Seeking warmth and thinking only of an appetising breakfast, I hastened to our front sitting room in my dressing gown, only to find Mr Sherlock Holmes, already dressed and immaculately groomed, deep in dispute with that same lady whose late husband had been a considerable force in City banking and Holmes had assisted in some fraud case. She lived at that most prestigious terraced address at the southern end of Regents Park.

"Your dog is really not within my province, Mrs Lodesley. A local policeman, or else a park attendant is your best shot to trace the whereabouts of your missing pet. I have only limited time and resources."

"I tried, I tried! I tell you, Mr Holmes, I've tried everything. I was taking my Scotch terrier for her usual walk in the park when she slipped her lead."

"Understood," sighed my colleague, giving me a withering glance before settling back in his armchair to smoke and read the newspaper.

Warming my hands before the blaze in the hearth, I felt mounting annoyance with his indifferent attitude. Where was the sense of urgency?

How could anyone not feel sympathetic towards this poor lady, her whole world just now shaken to the core? I believe, at that instant, she would have offered Holmes half a million in sterling to get her dog back. I exaggerate, of course, but it was piteous to witness her plight and not be able to offer much save kindly platitudes.

"I shall walk back with you, Mrs Lodesley. We can retrace your route across the park. Maybe someone will remember seeing your Scotch terrier in the gardens. Have you some important case then to attend to this morning, Holmes?" said I, rather tartly.

"I tried, Dr Watson, I really tried," Mrs Lodesley again insisted before bursting into tears. I did my best to console the woman, settling her down upon the basket chair closest to the fire, serving her a cup of coffee and plumping the cushions."

"Mrs Lodesley," asked my friend from behind his Daily Telegraph, "if I may be so bold, what was that piece of paper you were clutching so fervently when you entered the room?"

"Oh, I forgot." She dabbed her swollen eyes with my proffered hanky. "Mrs Merrit wrote me a message, my next-door neighbour, you know. How fast she attains her handwriting, scribbling loops, abstract jottings on a pad with her pencil that eventually turn into a fairly readable script. I was desperate, you see, anxious to find out where my dog has got to, so sought 'their' help."

"By 'their', I presume you refer to dead people?" said my companion, puffing on his pipe with total disinterest."

"Enlightened angels, high begotten guides I refer to, sir, not re-animated corpses," she answered, a trifle hotly, misunderstanding my friend's comments to be a criticism. She hastily passed across her note so that Holmes could better peruse its contents.

"Well, it appears plain enough. What do you make of these Egyptian hieroglyphics, Watson? I confess, I am unable to translate, however."

"Just that," said I, getting up and passing the single sheet of paper back to Mrs Lodesley, careful not to be insensitive and unwittingly cast some off-the-cuff disparaging remark about mediums of spirits. "Egyptian hieroglyphics? Did Mrs Merrit offer any clue to its meanings?" I asked guardedly, helping myself to more ham and egg, glancing out of the window at the frosty slate roofs and smoking chimney pots of the houses opposite. "Presumably, she possesses a gift for spirit writing, an ability to convene with the dead."

"This ancient language of the Nile was entirely new to her, Doctor. Mrs Merrit confessed she had never encountered such picture symbols before in her long mediumship."

"A pity. What can one do when faced with such an unsurpassable barrier? Now, if the message were written in plain English, we might be able to proceed."

"Well, we could venture to the British Museum," I suggested, by now bordering on becoming infuriated. "They have a Department of Egyptology, I believe. Are you really so busy and occupied at present on a case, Holmes, not to spare a morning or so to help Mrs Lodesley out?"

"Oh, very well." My companion, chucking his newspaper aside, leaned over and replaced his long cherry-wood pipe back in the rack. "Professor Neal is the head of department and I have not spoken to him in quite a while. Our baffling little line of Egyptian hieroglyphics shall brook some amusement anyhow. Now, Mrs Lodesley, you and your absentee Scotch terrier have our full and undivided attention for the morning."

————

To thus it was, upon that bright, crisp morning, not yet ten of the clock, a static chilliness resilient in the air, we summoned a four-wheeler and, bound for the British Museum with Mrs Lodesley, huddled anxiously in her furs, we quietly pondered the mystery of Mrs Merrit' s spirit writing.

Just after the crossroads to Bloomsbury Street, we paid our cabman his fair and made straight away up the steps of the museum, heading for the Department of Egyptology.

Professor Neal, in charge of the wealth of Egyptian artefacts and sarcophagi in Rooms 62-3 upon the upper floor, was delighted to see Holmes, who, at this juncture of his career, was regarded as something of a celebrity in certain intimate circles of London academia, and directed us into his office, alive with all the clutter of a head of department. My colleague was not long in getting to the crux of the matter, showing Neal the scrap of paper. I confess quite candidly, I was amazed when we actually got a serious measured response and were not laughed out of the premises.

"The line of hieroglyphics is genuine and refers to the joys of owning pets, in this case a dog, and the masters wish the dog should be embalmed and join him in Sett's tomb at Abydos springs to mind, his favourite hound being regarded as sacred and mystical was, after being poisoned, embalmed and wrapped in linen before being placed at the feet of the king inside the coffin."

"Have you an example of these pet burials we could look at?" asked Holmes.

"We do, but the rooms are at present closed for renovation. Old Griffin has a very splendid mummy case at his house containing the wrapped, embalmed remains of a pet dog and its owner, a wealthy cloth merchant called Elsaff."

"Sir Alexander Griffin, the respected Egyptologist and archaeologist so acclaimed for his digs at the Naquada sites of Qau El-Kebir and Matmar, that hoard of bracelets, beads of gold, carved hounds and lapis lazuli was surely worth a fortune, much of the treasure now on display here at the museum," remarked Holmes.

"Yes, we were very fortunate. Old Griffin's proved a great ally. The days of his great pioneering digs are over, of course, but at eighty-six, he's as mentally astute as ever, very friendly and always approachable, even though I hear he's in poor health. He made a great study of mummified pets and has even written a book on the subject. You'd best pop round and see him, Holmes, and show him this scrap of paper. He will be able to decipher and offer a better translation. Gordon Square, I've got his address somewhere."

———————

One block north of Russell Square, once in Bloomsbury, under lowering dark grey skies that threatened sleet or snow, our cab trotted to a standstill outside a very handsome Georgian residence and we lost no time in raising the servants. The bell-pull clanged and not long after we were met upon the step by the senior housekeeper who was wringing her hands and appeared most distressed upon some matter.

"Is Professor Griffin at home, perchance?" enquired my companion civilly. "We have come quite informally on a matter pertaining to his mummy case."

"I'm afraid Professor Griffin has passed away, sir. We have yet even to inform the undertaker, let alone his many friends and colleagues."

"I am a doctor," said I. "Would you like me to verify the cause of death? I can at least put your household at rest concerning certain medical aspects."

"His own personal physician from Harley Street shall be calling presently, but what harm can there be in an impromptu specialist opinion? I myself suspect old age alone was responsible for my dear master's demise. Perhaps you will confirm that, Doctor? Professor Griffin, although mentally alert at eighty-six, was in failing health since suffering his stroke last month. He could speak in barely a whisper, but his words were jumbled and his eyesight deteriorating. Do come in out of the cold, all of you. Please take a seat in the hall madam. Gentlemen, step this way, he is in here."

In that darkened, comfortably furnished room, curtains drawn out of respect, the cowering corpse sat stiff and dead before the fireplace, the deceased, pasty-skinned and fragile wearing a quilted smoking jacket and matching tasselled cap stared ahead with mouth agape, surprised beyond measure his life's work should be curtailed so abruptly, so finally, so irrefutably.

I carried out an examination of the old gentleman, but Holmes chose not to stay in the sitting room and retreated back into hall to join Mrs Lodesley. I was of course attended at all times by the rather formidable black-clad housekeeper, Mrs Ellingham - she that hovered behind me and watched my every move. After giving my prognosis that in every way agreed with her own - natural death caused from heart failure - I was surprised to discover, upon quitting the Gordon Square mansion and heading back out into the wintry cold, that in a very short space of time Holmes had managed to establish many discrepancies which he conveyed with great glee and enthusiasm to Mrs Lodesley and me as we rattled along in our four-wheeler, journeying our way back to Regents Park to search for that same lady's missing dog.

"You naturally observed the chair, Watson? That is of the most critical importance."

"what chair?"

"The chair old Griffin was sitting on, of course!"

"Well, it was of carved oak."

"And ... ?"

"Ran on casters."

"Bravo! I shall provide more succinct and detailed analysis. The chair in fact, Mrs Lodesley, was a swivel chair of the type that normally sits behind a study desk. You will note a sturdy oak piece with a revolving hub, carved arm rests and leather studded back - office furniture. You were also, I trust, aware of the deceased Egyptologist' s posture, dear boy? The right hand in particular."

"The arm was stretched out, certainly," I admitted, remembering the gnarled, stiffened hand clutching out at something.

"You will therefore recall the smudged third finger?"

"You infer Professor Griffin was holding a quill pen engaged in work of some kind - writing notes, for example. I've no argument with that, Holmes, although he was not sat at his study desk, was he?"

"He most certainly was, Watson, that is prior to him being wheeled hastily across the hall into the sitting room by a very worried second party hoping to revive the old gentleman by placing him better before the more lively fire of the sitting room than the practically extinct coals in the hearth of the study."

"So he was working."

"He was at the time scribbling this most excellent jumble of nonsense, Watson. The hour was late, the servants and that housekeeper, Miss Eilingham, abed. I conjecture old Griffin had agreed to meet with an American, most likely -who, I have no idea -and was engaged in communicating something of importance when he quite abruptly conked out. The resident mummy case, by the way, had, I observed, been opened and the bound relics of the mummified dog and owner tampered with, shifted roughly about."

"An American? How on earth do you deduce that, Holmes?" I asked with a frown.

"Two concise pieces of evidence emerged. I noticed, for instance, upon the corner of the study desk, someone had knocked out the ashes from their pipe. A very distinct make -a corncob, I might add, with a small, well-burnt bowl, an array of corn husk fibres mingled with the pile of ash. The coarse, rich mixture of tobacco smoke, the aroma of which still clung about the room, was clearly 'Olde Mayflower', a brand uncommon to Britain's tobacconists. Another clue - a very valuable Egyptian dish had, despite its rarity and great age, been rather thoughtlessly used as a spittoon."

"But you were only in that room for a few minutes," enjoined Mrs Lodesley, full of admiration for my companion's flare and audacity.

"Enough time to glean much useful data. While you, Doctor, were busy prodding and probing the corpse and that hawk-eyed housekeeper's attention occupied, I had, meanwhile, nipped across the hall and made a brief examination of the study. Sure enough, I did come across the scrap of nonsensical directions upon the desk atop of the blotter. Make of it what you will. Mrs Lodesley, let's hear your pennyworth. It'll take your mind off your dog."

"Well, Mr Holmes, written in a shaky hand it says simply 'the B.W.S. Is by my oath hidden in the - .' The writing abruptly veers off and we have blotches of ink. 'B.W.S.'? What in heaven's name does that refer to?"

"The quill pen had been dropped on the floor, I saw it for myself. Ah, here we are at the park. We shall leave our little puzzling 'B.W.S.' note for another time. Watson, Mrs Lodesley's dog must be our foremost concern for now."

I can report that during our extensive walk around the park, even taking in the edge of the zoo and the canal, Holmes remarked that the matter of dead Egyptian pets placed in sarcophagi might be worth developing.

Was, he proposed to Mrs Lodesley, her beloved dog in fact trapped inside some park hut or beneath the bandstand? The bandstand proved a dud, but taking yet another stroll around Queen Mary's Gardens, we spied in the distance on the grass a typical tea and ices open-fronted refreshment hut on wheels, left out of season during the winter with the metal shutter closed down and padlocked.

On closer inspection, hopes were raised, for it appeared the severe ground frost had caused the planking, which was so thick the dog's barking would be muffled, to expand, thus the kiosk door was wedged tight. Holmes and myself managed to wrench it open, and there inside we found the little terrier whining and scratching away with its paws.

What joy, what a wonderful reunion. I shall never forget dear Mrs Lodesley's cooings and endearments as she held her yapping pet once more in her arms. My colleague quickly deduced the dog must have got in through the partly open door when a passing, well-meaning groundsman or park attendant closed it tight, not realising the errant animal was within.

But to return to the main feature of this adventure we must go back to our familiar lodgings whence the following week, the first snow of the year having fallen and settled leaving an inch or so speckled upon rooftops and pavements along Baker Street, we received a surprise visit one afternoon from a tall, strikingly handsome and cultured American, a gentleman of middle years staying in London for a period of time.

"Mr Holmes, my name is Brad Griffin. I'm a lawyer from New York. Although long estranged from my father, the much respected Egyptologist, I received a letter from him asking me to come over to England at once, for he had suffered a stroke and was in poor health. Our meeting was to be kept entirely secret, and no wonder - back in those days of glorious plunder for the empire when, as an ambitious archaeologist, he was still making a name for himself, he and his cronies robbed a royal grave. The stolen find being no less than Princess Aesculapius' necklet of precious stones presented to her by King Solomon on her marrying one of his sons. Priceless Mycenaean and dug up in Nauplia. It would never have left the country and would be regarded as a national exhibit to be properly displayed in a museum. I think the old man felt guilty about his hoarding such a valuable relic, keeping it for himself to gloat over all these years."

"You will not be aware of this, Mr Griffin, but Dr Watson and I, accompanied a Mrs Lodesley, called in to see your father informally on quite an unrelated matter upon the morning of his death. Neal of the British Museum was patently unaware of the serious nature of his illness and recommended him to us. Interestingly, I was drawn to form certain tantalising conclusions. Pray continue."

"There was a scrap of paper -I've lost the confounded thing, or a maid threw it out. I was staying at the Langham at the time and, ·after wheeling my father into the sitting room, hoping to revive him and making a brief search of the downstairs rooms, I retired for the night back to my hotel."

"And presumably that same note left on the study desk, which I have here secreted in my pocketbook, had not the professor died, would have revealed the precious necklet's whereabouts."

"Hell, you're quick off the mark, but you're correct, and then allowed me to proceed with negotiations for its swift return to the rightful country of origin. What a damn shame the poor old guy died at the very moment he was about to write me where the necklet was hidden in the house. The stroke left my father unable to speak coherently, or in more than a jumbled fashion. However, he was just about able to put pen to paper. 'B.W.S.', incidentally, refers to Blackthorn Walking Stick, the silver engraved handle unscrews with a neat compartment inside for the necklet to be placed for safekeeping. That much I do know."

"Remarkable," said I. "That clever-handled walking stick is a prize worth finding."

"If only I knew where to find it! That's why I've come to see you, Mr Holmes. I'm damned if I haven't looked close on everywhere in that Gordon Square house at Bloomsbury, short of actually tearing up the floorboards. That night of the meeting, I even opened up the mummy case and had a rummage round inside, but discovered not a dime's worth. Now I'm officially staying at my pater's house in Gordon Square for the funeral and the will to be read, but despite offering a ten pound incentive to the servants and roping in Mrs Ellingham for a household search we found nothing."

My companion stretched his long legs on the hearth rug and, refilling his old black clay with tobacco, offered the Persian slipper to our guest who instantly retrieved a well-appreciated, if battered, corncob pipe from his coat pocket and took advantage.

"Very well, Mr Griffin," said he, lighting his own pipe with considerable panache. "I and my colleague Dr Watson should be willing to accompany you back to Gordon Square. Let us search out this Princess Aesculapius' necklet. Ha! If we managed to trace Mrs Lodesley' s dog in the whole of Regents Park, I see no reason why a valuable artefact should prove that elusive. Perhaps you would be good enough to write a list of the places already searched and a rough map of the downstairs rooms."

"Very well, Mr Holmes. Say, I'm real honoured to be associated with London's foremost consulting detective. Just wait till I get back to the States and tell the fellows at my club."

———

Our New York lawyer's unequivocal adulation of Holmes, although pleasing to behold, was a trifle premature. Brad Griffin was no doubt aware of my colleague's considerable fame both here and abroad through reading the various published accounts of his cases, but dare I say this, he had yet, unlike, for example, Inspector Lestrade or young Hopkins of the Yard, to actually encounter his radical and controversial methods first hand. That morning, I well concur both he and the retinue of servants' wits were sorely tested. After a long and intensive interview of each member of staff in the kitchen, which seemed to drag on for hours, Sherlock Holmes began a slow and methodical search of the lower rooms.

Some time later, he exclaimed to all and sundry towing along in his wake, "I shall require a shotgun." He lit his briar-root pipe and began pacing back and forth scowling at the walls and ceiling of the drawing room. "Ladies, cotton wool to be placed in your ears thus," he directed the servants.

"Do you intend to cause damage, placing the structure of this Georgian town house in peril, Mr

Holmes?" enquired a horrified Mrs Ellingham, doubting his very sanity.

"I do. The recovery of the blackthorn walking stick is paramount. All costs, including my expenses, will be met. Ah, Mr Griffin, you have found a suitable weapon -voila! Be good enough to draw back both hammers, old chap. Mrs Ellingham, you are clearly certain the painters and decorators were last here in August?"

"I have already gone over this with you umpteen times, sir. You interrogated us in the kitchen. I reiterate, the walls in the drawing room were repapered, the ceiling and surrounds attended to by painters and plasterers. Professor Griffin oversaw the work."

"Just so. Now close the door and stand outside, all of you ladies. Watson, and your too Mr Griffin, remain. Somewhere in this new decoration lies a weakness, a flaw. Let us lose no time in finding it!"

Holmes aimed the shotgun ceilingwards and fired. Such was the loudness of the explosive blast in that enclosed space of the drawing room that one of the windows blew out -and the trembling cut-glass chandelier clinked and chimed for a long time after. The shock wave, the intense reverberation shaking the room, proved highly effective in loosening a section of cornice along one edge of the ceiling, a hail of plaster and dust and fragments of mock-Georgian moulded grapes entwined with oak leaves showering onto the carpet.

But there was something else which came crashing down - a walking stick with a silver, unscrewable handle that had been cleverly concealed in the hollow of the length of cornice running round the top of the far wall.

Brad rushed across the room, kicking aside loose shards of fallen plaster before seizing the blackthorn walking stick in both hands and shaking it vigorously about. Gracious, one could hear stones rattling, clinking against each other inside the hollowed-out handle.

"Unscrew it - unscrew it!" Holmes exclaimed. Sure enough, once the silver engraved handle was twisted anticlockwise, inside was found the most exquisite piece of ancient Mycenaean jewellery to rival any on display at the British Museum. Princess Aesculapius' necklet was gloriously found.